I0689792

PROTECTING THE BRIDE

SHELLEY MUNRO

MUNRO PRESS

Protecting the Bride

Copyright © 2024 by Shelley Munro

Print ISBN: 978-1-99-106352-6
Digital ISBN: 978-0-9951395-8-9

Editor: Evil Eye Editing

Cover: Kim Killion, The Killion Group, Inc.

This book is a work of fiction. The names, characters, places, and incidents are products of the writer's imagination or have been used fictitiously and are not to be construed as real. Any resemblance to persons, living or dead, actual events, locales, or organizations is entirely coincidental.

All rights reserved. No portion of this book may be reproduced, scanned, or distributed in any manner without prior written permission from the author, except in the case of a brief quotation embodied in critical articles and reviews.

Munro Press, New Zealand.

First Munro Press electronic publication August 2021

First Munro Press print publication May 2024

DEDICATION

For Paul, my partner in crime and fellow adventurer.

INTRODUCTION

The wedding is off!

Curvy baker, Grace, kicks out her cheating fiancé two days before the nuptials. Unfortunately, her dream honeymoon is nonrefundable. She hates the idea of vacationing alone, but Cullen, her neighbor, suggests an alternative.

Military man, Cullen, has wanted Grace for years. During this furlough, he intends to move forward with his romantic plans. He's devastated to learn of Grace's impending marriage, then ecstatic on learning the wedding is off. Cullen seizes his chance, determined to woo the gorgeous Grace to his way of thinking.

The only problem is danger follows Grace on her fake honeymoon. While the military hottie is busy with seductive maneuvers, a menace arrives with his lady in their sights. It's time for this alpha hero to do his thing and protect the bride.

You'll love this friends-to-lovers romance because it contains a curvy jilted bride, the soldier from next door, a fake honeymoon, and lots of whipped cream and ketchup. Make of that what you will!

1

BAD NEWS FOR EVERYONE

"HEY, GRACE!"

The masculine shout followed by a sharp wolf whistle had Grace Feeney freezing in the middle of the footpath, near the bus stop. She glanced over her shoulder to see a six-feet-plus bearded man with shaggy brown hair bearing down on her. His faded jeans clung to the muscles of his thighs while a well-washed gray T-shirt—obviously destined for the rag bag soon—hugged his broad chest.

While she'd been gaping at the scruffy man, he'd used his long legs to cross the road and reach her side.

"Grace." The man's voice was softer now, his eyes a bright, sunshiny-day blue attracting her attention. "Put down your shopping and let me give you a hug."

It was the sight of his even white teeth and his husky voice that jogged her to sanity and rattled her memory back into sync. "Cullen?"

"Aye, it's me," Cullen said with a huff of indignation. He patted the region of his heart with his right hand. "I'm mortally wounded to learn you don't recognize the man you babysat all those years ago."

Grace rolled her eyes and attempted to rein in her smile. "You were ten, and in my defense, you've grown a few feet."

His eyes twinkled. "I know, but I like to tease you." His arms came around her in a tight, comforting hug the second after she set down her two canvas bags full of groceries.

She inhaled his fresh scent with a hint of citrus and laundry powder and savored the familiarity of his touch. When she'd seen him last—almost a year ago—he'd been clean-shaven with brutally short hair.

He pulled back with another flash of those white teeth. "I'm glad I spotted you. I've just done a run to the local dairy for a bottle of milk." He indicated the daypack he wore on his back that she hadn't noticed earlier. "Stocked up on some snack treats too."

Grace studied his features. Now that she knew his identity, she noted the minor details: the shadows of fatigue and the fact his smile didn't always reach his eyes. "How long are you home for this time?"

"Three months."

"Perfect timing," Grace said, forcibly halting her urge to caress his cheek and tell him he needed to sleep. Instead, she aimed for humor. "You can take care of my lawns for a change. That's if you don't have plans."

"You're going away?"

Grace cocked her head, their six-inch difference in height making this necessary, especially since she wore her work flats. "My honeymoon," she said, beaming at him.

His mouth dropped open for an instant, but he recovered fast. "I didn't know you were getting married. Who's the lucky man?"

"Jeffrey Howard. You won't know him since he moved to Papakura around six months ago. I met him during the time I was filming *New Zealand's Best Baker*. He's an accountant, and he works in Manukau. He—"

Cullen tapped her nose, and she ceased her chatter. "I still say you should've won that contest instead of coming second."

"My appearance in the final opened doors for me. I'm writing a recipe book, a bakeware store wants me to promo their special line of products, and I'm enjoying my job at the café. Jenny, my boss, lets me do what I want with the menu."

"I thought you wanted to set up your own place? The last time I was at home, you told me that was your dream."

Grace shrugged. It was still her goal, but Jeff had convinced her it was better for them to purchase an apartment in the city, that cafes and restaurants failed all the time. After consideration, she'd decided he was right, and it'd be wonderful to have a place in inner Auckland. It was an investment. "I still want to do that one day."

He nodded as if he was privy to her thoughts and agreed with her, but she also noted his sharp scrutiny, his brain busy dissecting her reply. She'd forgotten that about him—his keen intelligence. Most women looked at his pretty, striking face and sexy body, learned about his chosen career in the military, and misjudged him. They thought him only good for a jump in the sack, or at least that was what Cullen had told her last time he'd been at home.

"Will you invite me to dinner soon? I want to meet this fiancé of yours and make sure I approve of him before the wedding. Have you set a date?"

Grace grinned. "This coming weekend."

"Wow, that was fast." His expression blanked, which made it difficult to read his thoughts.

"Not really. We're both in our thirties. We love each other and don't see the point in waiting. I think you'll like Jeff. He's charming. Attentive. A supportive, intelligent extrovert and he encourages me to put myself out there. He wants to have kids soon." Although lately, Jeff had been cranky and dropped a few mean comments after working long hours. Problems at work, he'd told her when he'd arrived home and apologized with a bunch of spring flowers. She'd given him a pass since tiredness always made her snappish. No one was perfect. Grace noticed Cullen was grinning, and she pulled a face. "Sorry. Listen to me babbling."

"No, it's great to see you happy." He tugged her ponytail. "Where is my invitation?"

"I didn't realize you'd be home. I'll get an official invitation to you tomorrow. It's so nice to see you again, Cullen." Grace gave him another swift hug before stepping back. "I'll call you about dinner. Maybe in the next night or two?"

"Works for me," Cullen said and bent to pick up her shopping bags. "I'll carry these to the door for you."

"You're rockin' a mountain man look. I didn't recognize you at first."

Cullen grunted as he shortened the length of his strides to match hers. "The last mission required us to fit in with the locals."

"I see." Grace didn't ask for details. Cullen was tight-lipped about his job with the New Zealand Special Air Service. She no longer asked questions because he never proffered answers. All she knew was that his job was dangerous, and she gave a sigh of relief each time he came home in one piece.

Cullen handed over her shopping at the gateway. "I'd come in and bother you, but I'm meeting a friend for drinks."

"No problem. It was great to see you again. I'll check with Jeff about dinner and get back to you." Grace impulsively stood on tiptoe and kissed him on the cheek.

Cullen froze before stepping back, and Grace gave a small laugh to hide her sudden discomfort.

"See you soon," she said with a wiggle of her fingers. She walked up the flower-lined footpath—the purple-and-white pansies were gorgeous this year—to the front door of the house where she'd grown up and halted. A pair of sneakers balanced on the branch of the tree in front of her property. *Kids*. She wasn't getting out the ladder to retrieve them. If the owner of those shoes wanted them back, they could make the climb themselves.

She loved this house and hated the idea of selling it. Her

parents had moved into a lifestyle village and given her the property for a token amount. This suburb was vibrant, and she enjoyed living here since she knew everyone in the neighborhood and it was close to work. It was also on the bus route, which came in handy since Jeff had needed to borrow her car this morning. By the time she walked past a bed of purple and pink petunias and the hanging basket bursting with spring color near the front door, Cullen had disappeared.

His mood had been strange, and she wondered if he was meeting a girlfriend.

She paused on the step, surprised to find the door ajar. That was odd. She pushed the door open and peeked inside, but nothing out of the ordinary jumped out at her. When she cocked her head, she heard nothing except the tick of the clock in the nearby lounge. She stepped inside and let out a shuddery breath. Stupid door. She'd been in a hurry this morning, and she'd carried a container. In the future, she'd make certain she shut and locked the door.

In the kitchen, she set her shopping on the counter. She slipped her handbag off her shoulder and left it on the chair. Grace unpacked her groceries, placing the milk and other chilled items in the fridge. She ripped off the inner seal of the ketchup bottle and prepared the whipped cream for future use. She was about to place the items in the pantry when a foreign noise encroached on her awareness.

Was that a groan?

She took two steps in the sound's direction and came to a sudden halt. It wasn't wise to take on an intruder. No, she'd call the police. Grace retreated to grab her phone from her handbag. She tapped in her password and pushed one-one. She was about to tap the third digit of the emergency number when a woman shouted.

"Yes! Yes! Right there!"

When a masculine groan followed, Grace ended her call. She advanced another two steps before she decided a weapon wouldn't be stupid. At a loss for a suitable deterrent, she snatched up her ketchup and cream and marched toward her bedroom.

Her bedroom.

She paused in the doorway and gaped at her fiancé's naked backside and the slender and supple feminine legs wrapped around Jeff's waist.

Fury rose, and she clenched the bottle and can, wishing it was Jeff's neck she was wringing. The rat was cheating on her only days before their wedding.

How long had this been going on?

The woman screeched out her release. "Yes! Yes! Yes!" she shrieked, loud enough to raise the roof.

Grace's mouth pressed to a firm line. She recognized that seductive voice.

The couple collapsed to the bed, their breathing hoarse while the scent of their lovemaking filled her bedroom. She'd need to fumigate the place once she got rid of them.

The pair started kissing and moaning and groaning all over again.

Grace thumbed the flip top of the ketchup and yanked off the spray cream cap. Neither of the participants in the bed-sport heard the faint noises Grace made when she opened the bottles.

"I want to lick your dick and suck on it until you explode."

Grace calmly stepped forward and squirted the pair. She took great pleasure in spraying her next-door neighbor directly in the face with cream. While Julia spluttered and cursed, Grace doused Jeff with ketchup, receiving immense satisfaction from splattering him with the blood-red sauce. The cheating scumbag was lucky she wasn't going at him with a blade. The urge to do so trembled through her, because she possessed knife skills. The judges of the *Best Baker* contest had confirmed this fact on live television.

Julia squealed, the high-pitch cry hurting Grace's ears. The pair floundered around the bed, their bodies slippery with food substances.

"What the fuck?" Jeff spluttered, futilely wiping at the ketchup dripping down his cheeks.

"You should know, since you're the one doing the fucking," Grace said sweetly and shot him with a blast of cream and another of ketchup. "In my bed with my neighbor."

"He says you're like a plank of wood in the sack," Julia said.

"Really?" Grace used the last of the ketchup and cream, squirting Julia directly in the face before she focused on Jeff. "Get out of my house." She dropped her weapons and fumbled to get off her engagement ring. Tears formed in her eyes when the ring stuck on her knuckle. Long seconds later, she removed the ring and flung it at Jeff. It struck his oversize nose, and he let out a howl. Shot!

"Bitch," he snarled, gingerly touching his abused nose. "You've made me bleed."

Grace grabbed her suitcase, packed ready for their honeymoon on Stewart Island. "Make sure you're gone before I get back."

"Grace, this is the first time this has happened. It was her. She came on to me..." He trailed off with a shrug. "I'm just a man."

"Huh!" Julia snapped.

Grace snorted in concert with the woman. "Haven't got your stories straight?"

"Grace, we can fix this. It won't happen again. I promise you."

"Does exclusive mean nothing to you?" Grace demanded. "You asked me to marry you, told me you loved me, and in the next minute, I find you in bed with a...a...a floozy."

"Hey!" Julia bounded off the bed to grab her clothes. Ketchup and cream slid over her fake boobs and dripped to the floor. "I don't have to listen to your insults."

"You're the trespasser," Grace snapped and stalked away, wheeling her case after her. "If you're not out by the time I return, I'm calling the police."

"Please, I'm sorry. Grace, you can't do this." Jeff followed her from the bedroom, heedless of his nakedness.

"Just did."

Grace grabbed her phone and keys and kept walking, dragging her case with her. She walked out the door with Jeff shouting after her.

"You stupid bitch! You're boring in bed. Too

conservative. That's why I had to look elsewhere for a bit of action. I need an adventurous lover."

Fury gripped Grace, and the tears she'd been holding back with difficulty fled—to her relief. She whirled to face him. He looked ridiculous with the remnants of ketchup and cream decorating his person and his willy flopping around with each stomp. She couldn't help it—she laughed.

When he snarled at her, she gave him honesty. "If this is about me refusing to have anal, you're a dick. If you'd given me time, I might have agreed. You never gave me a chance."

"You're so self-conscious about your fat arse," he sneered. "Stop sampling those cakes you're always baking."

Grace stared at him. "You have the cheek to nag me about my weight. All those long lunches and dinners you've been eating are taking their toll. You're looking podgy there." She pointed at his stomach. "Doesn't go well with your skinny legs."

Julia strutted out, not appearing as well put together as usual. Her cream linen pants suit held red splotches, and she carried her strappy pair of black high-heels. They, too, bore clumps of red-tinged cream. "If this ketchup ruins my clothes, you can pay for the dry-cleaning."

Grace didn't bother replying to that bit of ridiculousness. "You're not welcome here. *Ever.* Don't let the door hit you on the way out. And you." She glared at Jeff. "The wedding is off. Get out of my house and leave my key on the kitchen counter. Let me know your forwarding address, and I'll send your stuff. I don't want to see you again."

With that said, she snatched up her handbag. She hauled her case outside and whipped across the lawn. Grace darted through the small wooden gate that connected her property with Cullen's. When she tapped on the rear door, and no one answered, she presumed Cullen had already left to meet his friend. He wouldn't mind if she left her bag there while deciding on her next move. Right now, she desperately needed a drink.

She glanced down at the uniform she still wore and pulled a face. It didn't seem right to grab a shower at Cullen's place, but she could change. Her honeymoon clothes. She'd purchased lingerie, jeans, blouses, and a couple of pretty floral sundresses and shoes. She'd wanted to feel attractive and good about herself. She'd wanted Jeff to be proud of the woman he'd married.

Now...

A tear slid down her cheek as reaction set in. Jeff and Julia had seemed comfortable as if this wasn't the first time they'd slept together. Now all those long days of work made sense. The weekends away, which Jeff had told her was a special task for a client. He hadn't liked to turn it down because the extra money would go toward their new apartment, and she'd agreed, admiring his dedication. She sniffed. At least she didn't need to sell the house any longer.

Whoa! The new joint bank account.

The thought galvanized her, and she sprang into action. She pulled a silky T-shirt and a denim skirt from the top of her suitcase. Confident she was alone, she stripped off her checked chef's trousers and her plain white T-shirt. Damn! She should've retrieved her car keys from Jeff.

If he took her car, she'd report him to the cops, but right now, it was more important to get to the bank and make sure her money was safe. She'd withdraw the entire amount she'd deposited on Monday and put it back in her private account.

Grace folded her work clothes and placed them neatly on top of her suitcase. She thrust her feet back into her work shoes and took off. Her car remained at the rear of her house, and she glimpsed a shadow in the kitchen. The ratfink. He was still there, despite her telling him to leave. If he thought to sweet talk her into taking him back, he could think again. Flowers wouldn't work.

There was no coming back from this.

Grace headed for the bus stop and timed it just right to jump onto the next one to get to her bank at Manukau. Once there, she joined the line of twenty-five—she counted them—and waited. Almost an hour later, she reached a female teller.

"I'd like to transfer money between my accounts, please."

"You realize you could've done this with online banking," the teller said in a tone not much above frigid. Her face was pale and drawn, and she pressed a finger to her temple as if she was suffering from a headache.

It was obvious she'd had a trying day too, so Grace inhaled and counted to five. She bared her teeth at the teller and hoped her expression resembled a smile. "I'm afraid the account is brand new, and we haven't set up online banking yet."

"You need to speak to a banking consultant," the teller said, grim-faced and impatient.

"No, not today." Grace intended to withdraw her money, and once she'd done that, she'd close the account. Thank goodness she hadn't agreed to give Jeff signing authority on the account where she received her wages each week.

"What is the account holder's name?"

"I have the account number here," Grace said and handed it over.

The teller hit several keys to punch in the number and did a slight eye roll. "How much did you want to transfer, and which account did you want it to go to?"

Every warning antenna in Grace went on alert. "Why did you roll your eyes?"

The teller averted her gaze. "I'm sorry," she murmured. "I shouldn't take my bad day out on you. The balance is twenty-nine dollars. How much would you like to transfer?"

"What?" Grace shrieked. "How much?"

Every eye in the bank landed on her. The security guard placed his hand on the radio transmitter at his hip.

"What did you say the balance was?" Grace demanded in a hoarse voice.

"Twenty-nine dollars and seven cents."

Grace swallowed hard. "I banked fifty thousand dollars into that account at the beginning of the week."

The teller frowned at her screen. "Yes, I see where you opened the account and paid in the first deposit. It appears someone withdrew fifty-six thousand dollars the following day."

"Fifty-six thousand," Grace whispered. "I didn't do that."

The teller sent her a look, and it bore more than a trace of sympathy. "I see there is another signatory to the account. You'll have to ask them about the withdrawal."

A sick sensation pressed against Grace's chest and dropped to the pit of her stomach like a hefty weight. "Perhaps I should speak to a banking consultant now. Could you arrange that for me?"

"I'm afraid you have to go to the desk over there." She gestured to the other side of the bank.

Something in Grace's expression must've tugged at the woman because she relented after a brief pause. "Wait there. I'll get someone to speak with you."

"Thanks," Grace whispered and closed her eyes, trying to contain the scream building at the base of her throat. She and Jeff had agreed they'd pool their resources to purchase the city apartment. They'd agreed to pay their savings into this account since they'd get higher interest with combining their income, and it'd be easier to apply for a loan to gain access to the rest of the purchase price. Jeff had told her he'd needed an extra week before his term deposit fell due and he could pay his money into the account. She'd trusted him, and she wondered if he'd ever planned to go through with the marriage.

Had this been his plan all along? Romance her, steal her money and get her to break off their relationship by making sure she found him with another woman.

No, that made little sense because she'd finished work early today. She shouldn't have arrived home for another two hours.

While she was waiting for the teller to return, she hit speed dial for Jeff. His phone went straight to voicemail, and she hung up without leaving a message. He'd know he'd missed a call from her.

The teller returned with a young man of Māori descent with closely cropped black hair and deep brown eyes. He wore a white business shirt with navy trousers and a plain navy-blue tie wrapped around his neck in a Windsor knot.

"This way, please," he said and showed her into an office. He gestured her to a chair and shut the door before rounding the desk to take a seat. "I understand the other account signatory has withdrawn the balance of the funds in your account."

"Yes." Grace clasped her sweaty fingers in her lap and tried hard not to cry. Given the panicked glances from the young man, he thought she might fail this mission. "Is-is there anything you can do? He didn't have my permission to take this money."

"I'm afraid there is little recourse. He is a signatory, which implies he has the authority to do whatever he wishes with the balance in this account."

Grace closed her eyes, her heart beating way too fast. Her entire savings had disappeared.

"I suggest you contact this person." He tapped on his computer. "Jeffrey Howard and ask him what he has done with the money. Perhaps this is merely a misunderstanding."

"No." Grace opened her eyes and straightened, her spine hitting the back of the chair. "He knew what he was doing."

Hindsight. What a wonderful thing.

"Is there any way Jeff can withdraw money from my other personal account?"

"Does he have signing authority?"

"No, thank goodness."

"As long as you don't give him your debit card and he doesn't know your pin number, you're fine."

Grace thought for a while. "It's possible he'd have an excellent chance of guessing my password. Is it possible for me to change it today?"

"We can do that right now."

Half an hour later, Grace left the bank on shaky legs. She wanted a drink in the worst way. After considering the possibilities, Grace decided not to buy a bottle of wine and drink on her own. She'd catch the bus home and go to her local for a few drinks. That way, she could check to see if Jeff had vacated her house, and if he hadn't, she'd march right up to the ratfink and demand he give back her money.

2

ENCOUNTER AT THE LOCAL PUB

"CULLEN! GREAT TO SEE you," Josh Williams said, giving him a man-hug and slapping him over the back the instant Cullen joined him at the pub.

The familiar scent of beer, a hint of BO from the beefy man perched on a stool at the end of the bar, and the fleeting notes of floral furniture polish and disinfectant wrapped around him, embracing Cullen with comfortable familiarity. Casual chatter floated on the air, the combination of New Zealand slang and Māori amongst the English words easing the tension in his shoulders. The everyday conversation was a welcome change from the war zone he'd departed earlier this week.

Cullen grinned at his friend, who wore a navy-blue T-shirt with a rip near his right armpit, a pair of faded blue jeans, and scuffed work boots. A cap advertising the World Rugby cup hid his close-cropped dark brown hair and a significant portion of his face.

"How is civilian life treating you?" Cullen asked.

He and Josh, along with Dillon, Josh's older brother, had been in the same NZSAS unit for a while until a reshuffle had Cullen transferring to another group.

"Let's grab a beer and a more private place to sit, and I can tell you," Josh said.

Cullen scanned the beer offerings at the bar, and his brows rose. "I've been away too long. This place used to sell two types of beer on tap."

"Mate." Josh squeezed his shoulder. "Every bar worth its salt sells craft beer these days. I haven't been here before, but I've been watching the customers while I've been waiting for you. It seems like a great crowd. I'm glad you suggested a place that was out-of-the-way. I get sick of people watching me."

Cullen barked out a laugh. "You shouldn't have married the big boss then." He kept his voice low because he didn't want to snare attention either. "This was always my local once I reached drinking age. Are you hungry? They used to do a tasty meal here, and I've been dreaming of a steak for the last week. I swear I could smell charred meat when I woke."

"Yeah, I understand that sentiment." Josh scanned Cullen, his gaze piercing. Knowing. "Difficult deployment this time?"

"Better now that I'm home for three months. Got some bad news, though." He gave his order to the lanky barman, and Josh did the same. "Is the kitchen open?" Cullen asked. "I've been craving a steak."

"Would a steak burger work?" the barman asked.

Cullen considered.

"Here's the menu. Come up to the bar and order when you're ready," the barman suggested.

Cullen handed over his credit card. "Keep it," he said. "I'd like to run a tab."

He and Josh found a secluded booth and slid into the seats. In the room next-door, the click of pool balls indicated a game in progress.

"Do people recognize you a lot?" Cullen picked up his beer and savored the crisp, hoppy taste of his first mouthful. "Is it difficult being married to the prime minister?"

"I used to fly under the radar more easily during Ashley's first term. Now that she's in power for a second, my life is more difficult. I have to plan ahead and take care when or where I meet with my friends."

"Like me?"

"Yeah, especially my friends who are still active in service. I'd hate the press to grab a photo of me when I'm with you or one of the others."

"I hear Frog married recently and has resigned."

"Yeah." Josh took a sip of his beer. "Did you know Frog can sing?"

"Were you drinking before you came to meet me?" Cullen demanded. "I've heard Frog at karaoke, and it was like listening to a bullfrog."

"I've heard him too, and he can't carry a tune to save himself, or so I thought. Turns out he was playing us all to provide moments of levity when we needed it. He sang at

21

his wedding and when he finished, not a sound broke the shocked silence. The man has talent."

Cullen laughed. "He's gonna dine out on that story for years."

"What will you do during your time off?" Josh asked, interest flaring in his blue gaze.

"I want to paint the interior of my house and update the kitchen. Other than that, I intend to chill. Maybe do some training to keep up my fitness."

Josh cocked his head. "What about the woman you told me about last time you were home?"

"That's the bad news. I'd hoped to push forward with that too, but she's getting married this weekend. Missed my opportunity there. Grace is six years older than me, but I've never met any woman who comes close to her. She's kind with a great sense of humor. And, man, she makes the best carrot cake I've ever tasted."

"She sounds like a mother," Josh said with a sly glance in Cullen's direction.

"Oh, she's sexy and looks nothing like my mother, nor I suspect yours. She's about five-six with one of those old-fashioned hourglass figures. She's insecure about her weight, and the clothes she wears don't always do her justice."

"And someone else scooped her up from under your nose?" Josh's voice held sympathy.

"Yeah. I didn't make a move before because I wasn't certain of my future or, given some assignments, if I'd even be alive for long. This last one was hell, and it made me think of Grace. I promised myself if I got through alive, I'd make a move."

"Sorry, man. That sucks," Josh said.

Cullen sighed. "Yeah."

"Maybe Ashley knows someone."

"No," Cullen said firmly. "No fixing me up with blind dates. I prefer to scout myself. Are you going to grab something to eat? How long can you stay?"

"Long enough for several drinks and to whip your arse in a game or two of pool," Josh said with a grin. "Ash is down in Wellington tonight. Some sort of emergency cabinet meeting. I have a security job tomorrow, putting in an alarm system for a toy millionaire. I don't suppose you want to volunteer to help."

"Are you willing to trade labor? How are your painting and sanding skills?"

Josh shrugged. "Sure. Why not? Dillon and Ella were talking about coming up to Auckland for a long weekend. Maybe Frog and Ada too. Ash and Ella were muttering about shopping, so you might rope in Dillon to help."

"It's not so much the help," Cullen confessed. "It's the company. If I'm not careful, I go into my head too much. It's not healthy."

Josh speared him with a thoughtful stare—one that sliced and diced and saw everything. "You understand your behavior. That's a plus."

With nothing more to add to the topic, Cullen picked up the menu and perused the offerings. "A steak burger and chips it is," he said, pushing aside the menu.

Josh picked it up with a decisive nod. "Works for me." He slid out of the booth. "I'll order at the bar. Want the same again?"

"Sure."

While Josh strolled off to the bar, Cullen mused about his bad timing. Rotten luck. Crap! He needed to suck this up and stop feeling sorry for himself. He should give up on Grace and move on. Maybe find an attractive woman and fuck away his frustration during his leave. That might work. He dipped his head in a nod of acceptance. A plan to fill his empty nights.

Josh arrived back with fresh beers. "The burgers will take ten minutes."

"No problem. Enough about me. How are you doing with civilian life?"

"My life isn't anything like what I imagined when I left the NZSAS. Frog conned me into keeping watch over his sister because someone was stalking her. We pretended to be engaged, and things went from there. Ash is a top lady even if we disagree on politics." Josh grinned. "Frog settled in Moewai, but he still trains for the Special Air Service. He, Dillon, and I invested in land down that way. We run sheep."

Their burgers arrived, and he and Josh continued catching up regarding friends and acquaintances. Cullen demolished his burger, and the meaty goodness fulfilled his craving for a regular steak. "I might eat here while I rip out my old kitchen units."

"Ash would like this place."

Cullen stood, grabbed their empty glasses. "Want another beer? I'll challenge you to a game of pool."

"Deal," Josh said. "Check out the woman at the bar. If

you have a thing for the old-fashion movie starlet, she fits the type to a T. See you at the pool tables."

Cullen whirled around to stare and did a double-take as he watched Grace down an amber-liquid—perhaps her favored Scottish whisky—and shove her glass toward the barman for a refill. Long strides took him to Grace's side before he even realized what he was doing.

"Grace?" When he saw her earlier, she'd worn her checked chef trousers and a baggy white T-shirt. His gaze skimmed her body, taking in her tight denim skirt and the form-fitting black-and-white T-shirt. He smiled on spotting her flat, practical shoes—the ones she wore to work, if he wasn't mistaken.

She swiveled on her barstool and almost fell off. Cullen grasped her by the waist to right her, her flesh burning his palms through the thin fabric. As she recovered her balance, her strawberry blonde hair brushed against his cheek. "Cullen?"

Her beautiful green eyes widened, and he stilled upon seeing the evidence of tears.

"What's wrong?"

Her backbone straightened, and her expression froze. "Nothing."

She didn't seem confident of the fact. "Have you eaten?"

"Not hungry," she snapped, lifting her dainty nose a fraction as if to say *none of your business*.

"If you keep drinking that way, you'll need food inside you." He kept his tone reasonable and non-judgmental. Hell, he'd deadened his woes with alcohol a time or two.

She averted her gaze, her shoulders and tits rising as she

inhaled and exhaled in a heavy sigh. "After I saw you, I was in my kitchen unpacking the groceries. I heard a strange noise, and for a moment, I thought I had an intruder. The front door was ajar, but nothing seemed out of place. I assumed I hadn't shut it properly because it's happened before."

"Did you call the cops?" Cullen demanded. "What did they say?"

"I started to call them, but I heard moaning and groaning. I went into my bedroom and found Jeff and the neighbor."

"Jeff?"

"My fiancé. Ex-fiancé."

"And Julia—the neighbor on your other side? Is she still living there?"

"Yes, that Julia."

"What were they doing?"

"What do you think they were doing? They were doing the naked mambo in my bed." She glared at him. "Fucking, in case you're in any doubt."

"Crap."

"Yeah, Jeff blamed it all on me and said it was my fault he had to look elsewhere because I'm introverted and not adventurous in bed. He disapproved of my behavior."

"What?" Cullen was having problems following this conversation. "What behavior?"

"I decided I needed a weapon when I went to investigate. Although I know how to use a knife, I figured that wasn't a sound idea, so I grabbed the ketchup and a whipped cream spray and crept into my room. I found them..." Grace paused and shuddered. "Well, anyway, I lost my temper and squirted them with ketchup and cream. Until that point, they'd been too busy to notice my arrival."

"Ketchup?" Cullen managed, trying not to laugh at the picture that formed in his mind.

"Yeah, and whipped cream. One of those spray cans. I made a mess of my sheets and mattress, but it's not as if I'd sleep on them again, anyway. I'll have to fumigate the place just to get rid of their sex cooties."

Cullen stared at her, the urge to control his laughter a real challenge.

"Jeff was horrid. I'd packed for our honeymoon, and I had to get out of my place, so I grabbed my suitcase and used my key to get into your house. I hope that's okay because I didn't know what to do."

"No prob," Cullen said. "You're always welcome."

"Barman, another whisky, please," Grace called. "And a glass of sauvignon blanc."

"She'll have a steak burger too," Cullen said when the barman arrived with the drinks. "You can put them on my credit card."

Grace picked up the shot glass and downed it in one gulp. She shuddered at the burn before turning to Cullen, her eyes shiny with unshed tears. "He took my money. All of my savings."

Cullen straightened from his lean at the bar. "He stole from you?"

She nodded, and he stared helplessly as one lone tear trickled down her cheek. She swiped it away, a touch of anger in the gesture.

"Did you report it to the police?"

"Can't. Well, I can, but I doubt the cops will charge him. He had signing rights on the account. We were each going to pay money into a joint account. A deposit for an apartment in the city." She shook her head. "He had no intention—no, that's not true. I don't know his intentions, but he withdrew my money the day after my deposit and never said a word to me. He never deposited the money he told me he planned to transfer. I trusted him, and now I feel dumb."

"It's not stupid to trust someone you love," Cullen said.

"Huh!" Grace snorted. "It's obvious he didn't love me. It appears Jeff was spinning me a line, and I fell for his charm and his flowers. I don't even know if he meant to go through with the marriage. Why are you here? I understood you were meeting a friend."

"I am. I did. My friend is here. Come and sit with us while we play pool. The kitchen staff will deliver your meal to the pool table area." He glanced at the lanky barman and received a nod. "Come on. Stop moping."

"Really?" Grace's brows rose, ire in her expression.

Cullen bit back another inappropriate laugh and leveled her with a steady gaze. "Can you fix any of your problems right this minute?"

"No, although I'd like to punch the scumbag in his tiny dick," she muttered fiercely.

A laugh escaped Cullen this time, and he caught the barman's grin before the guy behind the bar wiped his expression as clean as his counter. Cullen lifted Grace off the barstool and picked up her glass of wine before urging her toward Josh, who was waiting patiently at the pool tables.

"I don't want to be a bother," Grace said. "You play with your friend, and I'll stay at the bar."

Cullen hid his grin and decided Josh had heard Grace because the smirking man winked at him. "No, don't drink too much. You'll regret it."

"I'll be numb."

"And have a hangover in the morning," Cullen informed her. "You'll suffer needlessly. What you want is revenge. That will improve your mood faster than a hangover. Josh, this is my neighbor, Grace."

"I need the restroom," Grace said.

Cullen nodded. "Don't try to sneak out without saying goodbye. I won't be happy if you try that maneuver."

Grace reared back as if he'd hit her. "How are you going to stop me?"

"Next time I catch up with you, I'll spank that curvy backside of yours."

Her mouth dropped open, and she stared at him in apparent shock.

"Shut your mouth." He tapped her chin and smiled at her, way more cheerful now than when he'd first arrived at the pub. "Say hello to Josh."

Grace turned to Josh, apology set on her face. "I'm pleased to meet—"

Cullen spotted the instant she recognized his friend. She whirled back to Cullen. "I'm interrupting a work meeting. Sorry! I'll just...just head back to the bar and take my drink with me."

"Josh is my friend. We worked together. Army," he added in a brief explanation that short-changed the bonding that occurred when men worked together in danger. Josh was more brother than a friend.

"Cullen is right. We've been friends for years."

Grace glanced over her shoulder and leaned closer to Josh. She would've fallen flat on her face if Cullen hadn't grabbed her around the waist. Not that he minded. Any excuse to get close to his sexy neighbor.

"But you're the first man," she whispered, her voice way louder than she imagined. "You're married to the PM."

"Doesn't mean I can't be Cullen's friend too," Josh said with a broad grin.

Cullen would've been pissed with his friend's flirting if he didn't know how much Josh loved Ashley.

"Sit at this table," Cullen ordered. "Ah, here's your burger. Please, do me a favor and eat as much as you can before you drink more. Grace?"

"Yes, Cullen." She blinked at him like a sleepy owl.

Cullen wanted to cheer. He'd caught her checking him out. The sizzle that neither of them had ever acted upon still lay between them.

"You really know Cullen. I'm not butting in where I'm not wanted?"

Josh winked at Cullen. "You're wanted, sweetheart. Do you play pool?"

"Badly," she said, her tone more cheerful. "I'm much better at baking cakes."

"That's true," Cullen agreed. "Grace made the finals of *New Zealand's Best Baker* contest."

"That's why you look familiar," Josh said. "Ash taped that program and watched every episode. Ash thought you should've won."

"There! What did I tell you?" Cullen said, giving Grace a side-eye.

"Ash likes to bake, too," Josh said. "But she doesn't get much time these days. She made cheese scones for the reporters last week. She felt sorry for them when they were waiting outside the gate to get a photo of her baby bump."

Grace's brows rose. "Did they get their photo?"

Josh grinned. "No, she sent me out with the scones and to tell them she was staying indoors for the rest of the day and working. She is having terrible morning sickness at present, although it seems to last all day."

"Should you be here?" Cullen asked.

"Yeah, when I spoke to Ash on the phone, she told me to come. She says friends are important, and I would get in the way, hovering if I'd flown to Wellington with her. That's true," he confessed. "It's hard seeing Ash puking out her guts and looking so pale. I feel as if it's my fault."

Grace chortled. "Your wife has to accept half the blame."

"I won't be telling her that," Josh said.

"Sit, Grace," Cullen ordered. "Eat your burger."

"I don't need food. I wanna drink away my troubles," she muttered.

"Fine. It's up to you. Sit there anyway." He wanted to monitor her because the last thing she needed was to get drunk.

He and Josh started a game of pool.

"Is that her? The woman?" Josh murmured.

"Yeah."

"It's easy to understand your attraction. She's pretty. She's also funny."

"Yeah. I've always enjoyed Grace's sense of humor. Her fiancé stole money from her. It was her money, but he had authority to sign on the account. He withdrew the lot and didn't mention it to Grace."

"She should still file a complaint with the police," Josh said. "She could get the money back."

Cullen broke. The balls split apart with a loud crack as the white struck them, and one rolled into the side pocket. He studied the ball placement before he crouched over the table for his next shot. He glanced at Grace and relaxed when he noted her nibbling fries. Any food in her stomach would help. "I'll boot him out of her house if he's still there. He made her cry. I've never seen Grace cry."

"You have a plan?"

"Not yet, but I will soon. I need to discover what she intends to do next. Once I know, I'll start with my strategy to win her around to thinking about me in the romantic sense."

3

DROWNING SORROWS

GRACE STARED AT THE impressive steak burger and the surrounding thick-cut fries. Not even the meaty aroma enticed her appetite. How could she eat with a knot the size of Stewart Island sitting in the pit of her stomach? But she took Cullen's advice to heart. Drinking without taking responsibility rated as plain dumb.

Jeff had cheated on her with her neighbor.

Every positive characteristic she'd ascribed to him, had liked about him was a lie. Instead, he'd played her, and the knowledge increased her ire. *Idiot!* Excited to meet a fascinating man who'd shown interest in her, one who'd wanted a family as much as her, she hadn't questioned Jeff's behavior. His timetable had been all over the place, and she'd accepted his explanations, not once asking him for complete details.

No, not entirely true.

She had asked questions once when he'd come home smelling of heavy incense and amber—an Oriental fragrance she'd never wear because it had brought on a headache the instant she'd identified the perfume. Jeff had acted as if she was making a problem where there was none. Didn't she trust him? Later, he'd apologized profusely, saying the long meetings had made for little sleep, but he'd made her feel small and uncertain despite his explanation.

In hindsight, she should've asked more probing questions.

She hadn't truly wanted to move to the central city, nor to sell the house her parents had left her. Thank goodness she hadn't allowed him to talk her into listing her home with an agent. He'd hinted they should do that in the future but hadn't pushed.

Grace plucked a fry off the plate and absentmindedly shoved it in her mouth. Salt and oil burst over her taste buds as she crunched down on the fried potato.

One thing—she wouldn't miss the judgmental expression on Jeff's face whenever she ate. She'd tried to explain tasting and analyzing flavors was part of her job, but Jeff had chastised her for over-eating. Oh, he'd couched the comment as concern for her health. Nevertheless, it had still speared her to the heart. Defiantly, she shoved another fry into her mouth. The fry was crispy and evenly browned. The perfect fry.

She reached for her wineglass and took a sip. Yeah, too bad what Cullen thought, too. She was getting good and drunk. Grace gulped another slug of wine.

"Is that wise?" Cullen asked after he'd potted the black.

He reached over and shunted the plate of food closer to her. "Eat."

She glared at him.

"Don't you have wedding stuff to cancel? You'll need a clear head for that."

"No, I don't need a sober mind to do any of that." Crap. She should've thought of that first. She'd been so upset with finding Jeff and Julia together, then learning he'd taken her money. The wedding was in two days. No, dammit, she could cancel everything tomorrow. It was after hours, anyway. She bounded to her feet and strolled toward the bar, staggering the first two steps before she righted herself. A masculine arm curved around her waist, the heat of it searing through her silky tee. She gasped at the physical contact and the sudden yearning that clubbed her over the head.

"It's all right," Cullen whispered. "I've got you."

Grace straightened and yanked from Cullen's touch before she did something idiotic. "Please, just let me be."

Cullen finally nodded, although she had no inkling of what was going through his mind. "I'll be playing pool with Josh if you need me. But do me a favor—please eat the burger if you're going to drink more."

Grace studied him for a moment longer before jerking her head in affirmation. She shuffled back to the table and took a seat, the weight of a stare on her back the entire time. Grace scowled at the burger, and her stomach twisted. The last thing she wanted was to eat, but Cullen was correct. She picked up the knife and fork and poked at the top bun. She flipped it off and dragged out the steak. He was right about another thing. The meat was excellently seasoned and perfectly cooked.

Her mind drifted to the aborted wedding and the list of people she'd need to contact. Luckily, they'd kept the celebration small, but there were still fifty people on the guest list. While she'd done a lot of the catering herself and spent hours laboring on the wedding cake of her dreams, she'd still outsourced. Money lost since there would be no refunds at this late stage.

What a mess.

Grace ate the piece of steak and half of the fries before pushing away the plate.

She pulled a notebook out of her handbag and jotted a list. Telling her parents was going to be the worst thing. They intended to help with last-minute things. With a sigh, she pulled out her phone and composed a text.

Mum and Dad. Bad news. The wedding is off. I'm fine. Will call tomorrow.

Grace hit send and placed her phone on vibrate. Her mother would demand details, and right now, the subject was a gaping, raw wound. She'd been blind. An idiot. Admitting that to her parents… She exhaled. Jeff had acted so sincere, and he'd cared for her, but in hindsight, she'd missed the huge signposts in their relationship.

Until today, he'd seldom spoken a harsh word to her. Huh! He'd been too busy romancing her and planning to rip her off. It'd been in his interests to keep her on the hook, keep her sweet. It surprised her he'd let the wedding date get this close. A thought occurred. It was early last week when she'd agreed to open the joint account. She'd been so busy it'd been difficult to find the time to open the bank account.

Wow, she was so stupid.

He'd been biding his time until he could get his hands on her money. He hadn't cared about her and had never intended to marry her.

Her phone vibrated, and she hesitated before checking the screen. Her mother was replying to her text—a message in capital letters. **RING ME.**

Grace ignored the text and blinked hard to contain the tears stinging her eyes. The discarded burger bun blurred, and she screwed her eyes shut. She refused to cry over that man. Much better to focus on payback. That was a productive direction for her thoughts.

Her right hand tightened on the pen she held, and she forcibly made herself relax to ease the strain. No, revenge was a waste of her time too. A list. What did she need to do tomorrow?

1. Cancel the caterer.
2. Cancel the wedding celebrant.
3. Inform guests.
4. Return wedding gifts.
5. Cancel the hall rental.

The honeymoon. Grace paused. The trip to Stewart Island was nonrefundable. The area behind her eyes throbbed again, and she squeezed her eyes shut. When that didn't help, she reached for her wine and downed the contents.

She set down the glass and shoved her notebook and pen back into her handbag.

Nope.

Tomorrow would be soon enough to confront this shit-show that was her intended marriage to Jeff.

She stood and wandered to the bar. She awkwardly scrambled onto a barstool and waved her hand to grab the barman's attention. "Scottish whisky," she said. "D-double." Her tongue thickened, and she had difficulty forming her words. Too bad. She wanted this day from hell to end. The sooner she numbed her pain and injured pride, the better.

"SHE'S GONNA REGRET THOSE drinks come morning," Josh murmured.

Worry flowed through Cullen, but he held the emotion in check. "Yep, but sometimes you have to let people learn their lessons."

"True." Josh placed his cue back in the wall stand. "It's been great seeing you. Don't be a stranger while you're home. You're welcome to visit our place, or I can come to you. Ring ahead, otherwise the security team gets agitated. Sometimes I like to sneak around to keep them on their toes since it's my wife and child at stake should anything go wrong."

Cullen laughed. "I bet that goes down well."

"I warned them I'd test security. It's not my fault Ash's men ignored my comments. Dillon, Nikolai, and Frog were in our lounge having a beer before the security guys noticed. Man, it riled Nelson. He's the big Māori guy who has worked as personal protection since Ashley became the Labor party leader. I trust him and Gavin, Nelson's offsider, but the others don't have the same experience. Them, I like to test now and then." Josh's gaze drifted to Grace and the man who was chatting her up. "I'd better go. Do you need a hand to get Grace home?"

"Thanks, but I'll be fine. You ring your lady. When is the baby due?"

"Only six months to go."

"Is Ashley taking time away from her job?"

"Yeah, she's taking a month off after the birth. The deputy prime minister will stand in for her."

"Does she trust him?"

Josh flashed a grin. "Mostly, but don't quote me." He glanced at Grace again. "You sure you're okay with her?"

"Yeah." Cullen stood and hugged Josh. "It's great to see you, man. Time spent with people who get it helps."

"Took me a while to settle, but Ashley came into my life and needed me. Call me if you want to talk. If I'm not available, call Dillon or Frog."

"Thanks."

Josh thumped him on the back. "I like your lady. The canceled wedding is a sign. Don't fuck it up."

Cullen grinned, lifted a hand in farewell, and stalked over to Grace. "Cupcake," he said and placed his hand around her shoulders in a possessive statement. He angled his body a fraction and eyed the man attempting to make a move on Grace. "You busy making friends?"

Grace frowned, blinking at him. Oh, yeah, she was well on the way to drunk, and this guy was ready to take advantage.

"You ready to go home, cupcake? The babysitter will want to leave on time."

The balding man on the barstool next to Grace straightened. "You have kids?"

"Two boys. They're little hellions like their mother," Cullen said smoothly.

Grace's eyes opened even wider, and she swayed a fraction. "I-I-that's not true."

Cullen slapped his hand over her mouth before she blurted out anything else. "You'll understand I have to get my lady home."

"But I bought her drinks," the man spluttered.

Cullen stood straighter, rising to his full height and removed his hand from Grace's mouth. "Did you lead this man on?"

"No!" she snapped, spoiling her militant glare with a robust hiccup. She reached for her glass and swallowed the last of her wine, hiccupping again. Wine sprayed across the bar and the man's shirt.

"Time to get you home, cupcake." It wasn't far from her house, and he could carry her, but she might get upset if he carted her out of the pub in that manner. "Grace?"

The balding guy retreated with a peeved expression. He'd thought he had a sure thing in Grace, and Cullen was glad he'd been there to step in even if his interference irked her. The barman had kept a close eye on Grace, which Cullen appreciated.

"Don't wanna go home," Grace muttered. "Not a child."

"You're acting like one," Cullen countered. "Come on. Time for you to go home." He glanced at the barman. "Grace is my neighbor."

The barman nodded. "Thanks for taking care of her."

Cullen gave a head jerk in response and lifted Grace off her barstool.

"No," Grace shrieked, drawing attention.

Cullen whispered to her, his mouth hovering near her ear. "Do you want to add an apology to your list for tomorrow? You continue like this, and you'll be too embarrassed to come back here. A pity because as local pubs go, it's great."

"Stop," Grace said, still wriggling.

Cullen sighed. "I was trying to avoid a scene." He lifted her with ease and draped her over his shoulder, then grabbed her handbag. "Time to go home, Gracie." Long strides took him to the door, and Grace fought him the entire way, screeching at him to let her down. "You wriggle much more, and those men over there will get a fine view of your bared backside."

"What are you talking about?"

"They'll see me spanking you."

"You wouldn't."

"Try me."

Grace spluttered and fell silent as Cullen stalked out the door, held open for him by the helpful barman.

"Thanks," Cullen said. "Appreciate it."

The walk home was considerably quieter.

"I feel sick," Grace said without warning.

Cullen let her down and directed her to a leafy bush. She

fell forward on her hands and knees and vomited her heart out. Cullen lifted her hair out of the way and waited for her to finish.

"Okay?" he asked after a long period of silence, where she hiccupped once and breathed hoarsely through her mouth.

"Yeah." She wiped the back of her hand across her lips.

Cullen helped her to stand, and this time supported her with an arm around her waist.

"Sorry."

"No apologies necessary." Cullen guided her down a side street and directed her toward an alleyway that joined two roads and exited on a reserve near their homes. When they left the alley, Cullen spotted a car parked outside Grace's house. Instinct had him halting in the shadows.

"What is it?" Grace asked, swaying on her feet.

Cullen hauled her against his side to provide her greater stability.

"Shush." Cullen couldn't tell what had caused him to stop, but something struck him as odd. The vehicle idled as if waiting for someone. A man exited the car and melted away into the shadows. They were too far away for Cullen to identify or get a description. "Do you know that car?"

Grace glanced in the direction he pointed and blinked several times. "Which car?" she asked finally. "There are three, and they look almost identical."

Cullen held back his laughter with difficulty. His cupcake was well and truly sozzled.

The car pulled away from the curb, did a three-point turn, and drove away, disappearing into the darkness.

Cullen nudged Grace into motion, and soon they arrived at her house. A light shone in her bedroom, and another in the kitchen. Through the window, Cullen watched a man cross to the fridge and open it to study the contents.

"Your man is still in your house," he said.

"Not my man. Not any longer. Hate cheaters. Refuse to marry one."

"Good for you," Cullen said. "No problem, you can stay with me tonight, and tomorrow, we'll see about getting him to leave."

"Bastard," she muttered.

Cullen stilled, then realized she didn't mean him. She was talking about the cheater, and he agreed. The loser hadn't understood the treasure he'd had in Grace. He'd tossed her away without a second thought. Cullen wasn't stupid. He knew a second chance when it stared at him, and he wasn't about to waste his opportunity to win Grace.

Only a fool would let her go twice.

4

THE MORNING AFTER

THE *THUMP-THUMP-THUMP* OF A jungle drum woke Grace. She stirred, her head shifting a fraction to release the taut pull of her hair. Immediately, jagged pain pierced her skull, advising her to exercise caution. She swallowed hard and discovered her mouth was as dry as an Auckland dam during a drought. The room—perhaps a bedroom, since the softness of a pillow cushioned her head—lay in complete darkness. Cold pushed goosebumps across her bare arm and leg while heat seared her back.

Cautious about setting off the excruciating spikes in her head again, she used her other senses. The sweet, spicy, and faintly musky aroma scenting her mindful breaths wasn't familiar. Jeff didn't—

"Go back to sleep. It's still early," a masculine voice whispered in her ear.

Grace shrieked and whirled, her legs tangling in the

covers. Panic roared through her while lights flashed behind her eyes and resounded through her brain. *Bang-bang-bang.* She groaned.

"You gonna be sick, cupcake?"

Only Cullen called her cupcake. Instead of relief, his presence raised more quick-fire questions. What was she doing with Cullen? She slapped her hands over her chest, relieved to find herself clothed, although what the devil was she wearing?

"Why are you in bed with me?" she demanded.

Cullen rolled away. A bedside light flicked on, and she reared back, raising her hands to shutter the brightness.

"You're in my bed," he said, and it was difficult to ignore his smug amusement.

"What?" That'd be why she recognized nothing and why she felt so discombobulated. "Why?"

"Do you remember last night?"

Grace peered at Cullen's bare chest. Muscles. Gorgeous, touchable muscles. She swallowed hard and averted her gaze downward. *Whoa!* More skin. "Are-are you wearing anything?"

"My birthday suit," Cullen said. "I dislike sleeping in clothes."

"Oh." Grace shifted her gaze to the pale blue sheet that rode low on Cullen's abdomen. She gasped and wrenched her unruly eyes off the expanse of tanned male skin. Her head jerked upward. Ow! *Thump, thump, thump. Bang.* Grace cradled her skull and willed the throbbing to cease.

"Problem?" His voice radiated mischief. No doubt, those baby blues of his would gleam in concert as they did

45

whenever he teased her.

"*Noooo*," she said, frowning. Sluggish thoughts took time to slot together until her mind seized on one jigsaw piece.

Oh, yeah.

Jeff.

She'd caught the ratfink having it off with her neighbor. The wedding was off.

Today, she had to fix the mess that came with canceled nuptials. But that didn't explain why she was in Cullen's bed.

"Why am I in your bed?" She scowled at him when he merely lifted a brow. While she'd been out of it, he'd tamed his beard. Now he wore designer scruff rather than sporting the mountain man version. It made it easier to spot his masculine arrogance. Grace sniffed and raised her chin. "My mind is a little fuzzy about yesterday."

Cullen had the gall to grin. "You walked in on your boyfriend—fiancé—with your next-door neighbor."

"Yep, remember that part. Unfortunately," she muttered. "What happened after that?"

"You stopped at the pub and got drunk."

"But I don't drink. Not much."

"You did last night. Glasses of wine with fine Scottish whisky chasers."

"Oh." That accounted for her pounding headache. She never mixed her drinks and limited her intake because she didn't cope well with alcohol.

"When we arrived home, your fiancé was still in your house. I figured it was better if you stayed with me rather than encounter him. You need to be sober for that meeting since he ripped you off and stole your money."

Heck, yes. She remembered that part. *The bastard.* "Is he still at my place?"

"Don't know." Cullen stretched his arms above his head, and her gaze followed the graceful move like a tame puppy. She stared, drank him in because he was so pretty. Were those muscles as hard as they appeared? Her mind roared toward lusty sex, and she silently willed the pale blue sheet to slip lower, just to appease her curiosity.

Cullen's earthy chuckle jerked her to good sense. Grace averted her gaze, but not before she glimpsed knowledge and amusement in Cullen. Carnal knowledge.

Grace! What are you doing? You babysat this man.

She wrangled her gaze when her inner wild child teased her with a second peek. Grace rubbed her cheeks, suddenly adrift. This wasn't the way she'd envisioned her life. She wanted marriage and a family, and Jeff had made her believe he'd coveted those same things. A dog and a house in the suburbs—eventually. Camping trips during the summer holidays. She ached for the carefree fun she'd had as a child when she'd raced around the countryside with her cousins. Her grandmother had taught her to bake, and life had been so simple.

Now, she was thirty-something with a failed engagement and no money because the creep had stolen from her too. Maybe she needed a Plan B.

"I need to find a sexy man and have a passionate affair. Have sizzle-your-socks kind of sex and enjoy myself. If that even exists," she muttered to herself.

Cullen propped himself up on his elbow and regarded her with amusement. "There is so much to unpack in that statement."

Grace pressed her lips together and ignored him. "I'm getting a glass of water."

"I'll make coffee." Cullen moved as if he was rising too. The sheet covering his lower half slipped dangerously low.

"No," Grace shrieked. "Stop. Don't move."

His blue gaze fixed on her. "Why?"

"You're naked!"

"Yeah, so are you under that T-shirt."

Belatedly Grace became aware of her unbound breasts and the air circulating her nether region. "What? How?" *Why?* That was the question that grabbed her most of all. She always wore panties under her nighties. It wasn't as if Jeff noticed what she was wearing to bed, which should've been a big sign right there. *Gah!* She was such an idiot.

Another question occurred—one that required an immediate answer. "Who undressed me?"

His eyes smiled when he spoke. "I did because your coordination was off, although you did your best. Well, I removed your outer layers because you'd vomited on your T-shirt and skirt. You wrangled yourself out of your underwear. Something about plain cotton not doing it for you any longer. You told me you were donning your sexy stuff in the morning."

She hid her face in her hands, and the heat that suffused her cheeks was nuclear-hot. "You saw me naked?"

"Yup. Why are you hiding, Gracie? Your breasts are gorgeous."

"Gah!" she half-shouted as she rose with caution. Once clear of the covers, she tugged down the T-shirt she was wearing. It barely covered her arse-cheeks. Mortified, she scuttled to the toilet and took care of business. In the bathroom, she stared at her raccoon eyes. Sighing, she did her best to wash her face.

Cullen appeared in the doorway, fully dressed and carrying a robe. He handed it to her. "Why don't you take a shower? You'll feel better. Clean towels are in the cupboard there. I'll be in the kitchen."

"My suitcase is in the laundry." She had difficulty meeting his gaze. His genuine smile and easy humor at her expense didn't help.

"I'll bring it up for you and leave it in the bedroom."

"Thanks, Cullen."

His brief nod told her he understood she was thanking him for everything he'd done last night. He disappeared, and she closed the door. She considered locking it but decided that was overkill. She trusted Cullen implicitly, and while he was happy to tease her, he'd never cross the line between right and wrong.

Cullen was correct. While her headache remained, the hot water eased her fatigue. It couldn't, however, scrub away her embarrassment at her behavior. Grace gave a heartfelt groan. She had so much to do today, all of it horrid and mortifying. Once she'd dressed in shorts and a tee—again new clothes—she picked up her phone to discover messages. Many texts and voicemails.

Grace inhaled and dialed her mother.

"Hey, it's me," she said when her mother answered.

"Grace, are you all right?"

"I will be."

"What happened?"

"He cheated on me. I caught him in bed with another woman," Grace said, not sugarcoating the truth.

"Do you want us to come home to help?" her mother asked.

"Thanks, but no. I have a week off work, so I'll take a break."

"You shouldn't be on your own," her mother said.

"Mum, I'm not suicidal. Sure, I'm sad, but mostly, I'm angry at myself for making a stupid mistake and trusting him."

"On the plus side, at least you found out before the wedding. That makes things simpler."

"Yeah," Grace said, her mood turning bleak.

A quick tap on the door heralded Cullen's arrival with a cup of coffee.

"Thanks," she mouthed. "Mum, I'll be fine, although if you could spread the word to our side of the family about the wedding cancelation, I'd appreciate it. You still have the list of the guests?"

"Yes. Yes, I'm happy to do that for you. Really, Grace. Dad and I should be with you to help with the other details."

"Mum, honestly. I'm fine. I *will* be fine. If you could contact those on the list for me, that's all I need. Tell them I'll return the wedding presents soon. That it's on my to-do list."

"Oh, Grace. I'm so sorry." Her mother hesitated. "Your

father and I never thought Jeff was good enough for you. Oh, he was charming, but this cheating behavior shows we were right to worry."

Grace gritted her teeth and did a swift count to ten. "Hindsight is always easy. Mum, I appreciate your help. I'm going to keep my phone turned off. Text me if you need me, and I'll call back."

"Are you truly okay?" Now her mother sounded worried.

"Yes. I'm an adult, and I won't do anything stupid. Bye, Mum."

She hung up and turned off her phone before it rang again.

Cullen cast her a sympathetic look. "That bad?"

"Yeah. Evidently, Mum and Dad didn't like Jeff but didn't tell me."

"I'm sorry. That must suck. How are you? Really."

"Now that I'm over the initial shock, I'm pissed. And I feel stupid because Jeff conned me. If he didn't want to go ahead with the marriage, I wish he'd told me."

Cullen's big shoulders—still bare—moved in a shrug. "Do you want something to eat?"

Grace shuddered. "No. Definitely not."

Cullen nodded. "Scuzzball is still at your place."

"Really?" Grace scrambled to the bedroom window and peered outside. "Oh!"

Jeff was sitting on the deck with a coffee and his feet up. He'd propped his phone between his shoulder and his ear, and his casual repose indicated he had settled in for the duration.

"Bastard. He's carrying on as if he's done nothing wrong."

"What are you going to do?"

"I'll wait until he goes out and get the locks changed. That should work."

"After you've had your coffee, we'll buy new locks for the front and rear doors. I can change them for you."

"Are you sure?"

"It will give me immense satisfaction to lock the idiot out of your house," Cullen said. "Have you drunk your coffee? I'll make you another one, and you can keep me company while I eat breakfast."

"I need to ring the caterer and the marriage celebrant. The hall owners, etcetera."

"You can do that downstairs while you have another coffee or at least a glass of water. You'll be dehydrated after last night." He eyed her closely. "Do you still have a headache?"

She nodded and immediately wished she'd used her words. "Yes."

"Headache tablets are downstairs," Cullen said and walked out.

Grace stared after him. Some lucky woman would explore all that golden, masculine real estate. She sighed, picked up her empty mug, her phone, and handbag, and followed Cullen downstairs.

The scent of coffee and the inaudible rumble of the radio newsreader led her straight to the kitchen. Although finding her way around his home wasn't difficult. It was a replica of hers because the same builder had constructed both houses. Cullen took her mug, poured her a refill, and handed her a glass of water and two painkillers. A few minutes later, he placed a plate of toast and honey in front of her.

"Eat at least one piece for me," he ordered. "It will settle your stomach."

"Thanks." Grace studied her list—the one she now recalled writing at the pub before she'd drunk enough to sink a battleship. Or at least it felt that way. Now that she'd had a shower and drunk coffee, her headache had lightened to a dull throb. She inhaled, the scent of toast, butter, and sweet honey enticing her to try a piece.

"Good girl," Cullen murmured.

She stopped with the toast halfway to her mouth. Honey dribbled over the edge of the bread. A lightbulb moment. Cullen encouraged her while, more recently, Jeff would've made a comment about her ample backside and cutting back on calories for her health. She bit into the toast and savored the crunch of the bread and nature's sweetness. Delicious. She ate the rest of the piece before she wiped the honey off the counter and licked her finger.

"Grace." Cullen's husky voice jerked her gaze in his direction.

"Yes?"

"Don't let that bastard get to you. You are a sexy, vibrant woman. Don't let his shortfalls ricochet back at you."

"Um, okay." Grace didn't understand the gleam in Cullen's eyes. No, not quite true. It resembled desire, but she was misinterpreting the situation. Obviously. Cullen didn't think of her in that way. They were friends.

Nothing more.

She mentally shook herself and returned to her list. Time to get this show on the road. The phone calls became easier as the morning advanced. She didn't give full details, despite pointed questions and rampant curiosity. Instead, she ran with the highlights: the wedding was off, and she needed to cancel. What costs did she still have to pay?

In most cases, the answer was the full price, but she'd expected this reply. Luckily, she'd set aside money, and Jeff hadn't got his grubby hands on that account. To think she'd believed him when he'd told her he'd contribute a larger portion of the apartment deposit if she paid the wedding costs. At least she hadn't accepted money from her parents. That would've made the situation so much worse.

"Thank you," she said to the marriage celebrant. "My apologies for the inconvenience. I'll pay your account this morning."

"I'm sorry," Cullen said once she'd hung up.

"Not your fault. At least most people have been understanding."

"It helped that you're paying them," Cullen stated. "That bastard shouldn't get away with this."

"He has done nothing illegal," Grace said. "Immoral, yes, but nothing against the law. I'm lucky I caught him before the wedding. If I hadn't discovered him with Julia, I would've gone through with the marriage."

A vehicle pulled up outside her house, and Cullen stood to see what was happening.

"He's going out with a friend. Some guy," Cullen said.

"At least he's not taking my car, which is what he normally does." Probably out of petrol. A bit of a bugbear with Grace because Jeff seldom filled up with gas after he'd borrowed her car.

"Right." Cullen cleared the table. "Let's get those locks changed before he returns."

Grace stared at the empty plate in front of her, surprised she'd eaten all the toast. Cullen had been right. The nauseous sensation in her stomach had subsided after food and coffee.

"Have you finished your phone calls?"

"One more," Grace said, wrinkling her nose. "The honeymoon."

"You can call them on the way to the hardware store."

Cullen guided her from his house and opened the door to his garage. His glossy black SUV sat there, ready for his use. He opened the passenger door and lifted her into the seat before she could do it herself. Breathless, she fastened the seatbelt.

"Why are you so handsy lately?" She dialed the travel agent.

"You're a beautiful woman. I like you," Cullen said as he backed from the garage.

"I don't know what to make of that. Ah, Karen. Hello." Grace told her story for what felt like the *nth* time.

"Aw, Grace. I'm so sorry to hear that," Karen said. "The package and the airfares you brought aren't refundable. Remember? I did tell you. You'll have to use them or lose your money, I'm afraid."

"Oh, yes." Grace closed her eyes, suddenly wanting to

cry again. "Thanks for letting me know."

"Do you want me to cancel?"

"No, not at the moment. Thanks," Grace said and ended the call.

Cullen pulled into the car park at the local hardware store. "Something wrong?"

"I can't cancel the honeymoon."

"Where were you going?"

"Stewart Island. I've always wanted to visit. Jeff didn't seem to mind where we went, so I booked a week. The lodge room I reserved is expensive, but I figured it was a once-in-a-lifetime trip worth the extra expense. None of the holiday is refundable. Karen pointed it out when I booked, but I didn't care because I didn't foresee any problems. I booked the package, anyway."

"You should still go," Cullen said. "Especially if it's your dream destination."

Grace shrugged and climbed out of the vehicle. "I'll worry about that later. Let's buy the locks and get them changed. Crap, I don't even know which ones I need."

Cullen joined her on the walk to the store entrance. "Never fear, cupcake. I know the right ones." He urged her in front of him and directed her to the correct aisle.

The lock price had her cringing, but she sucked it up and presented her credit card. Soon, they were driving back to her place.

She'd wondered if Jeff might return before them, but all was quiet when they walked into her house.

"I'll start work," Cullen said.

"Thanks. What a jerk! The place was spotless when I

stormed out yesterday afternoon. All his gear is here." She stared at his clothes—a T-shirt, a pair of cartoon boxer shorts, and a shirt draped over the back of her couch. Fury sparked life in her, and she stomped to the kitchen for rubber gloves. She wasn't putting up with Jeff's crap. If he wouldn't leave, she'd make it easy for him and stack his possessions out on the curb. It was too bad if something happened before he arrived to collect them.

5

WEDDING FALLOUT

CULLEN REMOVED THE OLD lock and had to jog to his shed to collect his toolbox. On his return, he met Grace at the door, her hands full of bulging plastic bags. She lifted her chin and stalked past to dump her load at the curb. After wiping her hands on the seat of her shorts, she stomped back inside, returning a few minutes later with another armful of stuff.

"Is that the jerk's?" he asked.

"Yep, I don't see why I need to store his possessions."

Cullen stifled a grin. Several strands of her hair had come loose from her ponytail, and her cheeks were rosy with temper. This close to her, he caught a hint of citrus—either shampoo or body lotion she must've had with her in her suitcase. It reminded him of his grandparents' orange grove. Happier, more innocent times. Her indignant huff drew him from the memory.

Today, Grace wore a tight pale blue shirt that showcased her curves beautifully and a pair of black arse-hugging shorts that displayed her pale legs. On her hands, she wore bright pink rubber gloves. Everything about her drew him—her natural beauty, her grumpy expression, her body. Definitely, her curvy body, but she wasn't ready to hear him yet.

He needed to bide his time.

"Fair enough," he said, standing aside for her to storm past him again.

He finished the second lock at the rear of the house and checked the window security before searching for Grace. He found her in her bedroom. She had her back to him and was grunting while trying to manhandle the queen-size mattress off her bed.

"What are you doing?"

Grace let out a shriek and dropped the mattress. She whirled, tear tracks marking her cheeks. The knowledge of her crying struck him in the gut. He hated seeing her pain, although he couldn't be sorry she'd cut the jerk loose.

"I can't sleep on this mattress. I refuse. I'm putting it at the curb with Jeff's things. He can take it with him. I've already had to throw away my favorite set of Egyptian cotton sheets. They're ruined."

Cullen studied the greasy-looking stain. It bore a red tinge, but it wasn't blood. "What is that?"

"Remember, I told you I grabbed the closest weapons to hand? My ketchup bottle and UHT spray cream. It seeped through the sheets to the mattress. Jeff didn't even bother to strip the bed. He must've slept on the couch."

"I can take it out for you," Cullen said. "You grab the rubbish bags with the linen and any of his other belongings."

"Thanks," Grace said and hustled around the room, snatching up items and stuffing them into the rubbish bags. She hauled one outside and strode back to get the other while he maneuvered the mattress down the stairs. She'd made two more trips by the time he dragged the mattress to the end of the driveway and dumped it next to the pile of bags and trash sacks.

Each time a car drove past, it slowed, and Cullen would've bet the neighbors hovered at their windows, getting an eyeful of entertainment. On his return, he found Grace still in the bedroom, busily clearing drawers.

"How many clothes does Dickhead need?"

"More than me," Grace said, not stopping. "He said his job means he has to dress smartly."

"Did you tell me what he does for a job?"

"Accountant. He has big clients in the city, so he wanted us to buy an apartment there. He goes on a lot of business trips, both in New Zealand and Australia. Sometimes, he flies to Thailand, but mostly, Australia."

"You never went with him?"

Grace shook her head. "Whenever he asked me, I had work." She pulled three figurines from a cupboard and placed them on a side table.

"There were four. I wonder where the fourth one is. Ah, it's tucked under a pile of books."

"What are they?"

"Jeff bought them on one of his overseas trips. They

amused him. He had them on display for a while. They're a play on hear no evil, see no evil, speak no evil, except they look like gnomes instead of the usual monkeys. The fourth gnome had its finger raised in a royal salute. Jeff decided they were cute. I think they're a bit creepy." She picked one up and studied it closely. "You know, I might keep this one as a reminder not to believe everything a man says."

Cullen shrugged, once again suppressing his burst of humor. He enjoyed this feisty version of Grace. "If that makes you happy. Anything else you need shifting?"

"No, I'll be fine. This is the last of Jeff's gear."

"What are you doing about the Stewart Island trip?"

"I'm not sure yet. I'll decide today," Grace said.

"Call if you need anything." Cullen dug into his pocket and pulled out two sets of shiny silver keys. "These are your new keys."

"You keep one and leave the other for me."

Cullen nodded. "Make sure you keep the doors locked in case Jeff returns."

"I will."

They paused when a car halted outside.

Cullen stalked to the window. "People are helping themselves to the idiot's stuff."

Grace sniffed. "Tell someone who cares." She returned to her drawer rummaging.

Cullen wanted to pump his fist and cheer. He didn't. Instead, he said, "Have dinner with me tonight?"

Her hands stilled, and she glanced at him. "Dinner?"

"Yeah, we both have to eat. We might as well do it together."

She sat back on her heels. "You know, there's an Italian place close to here. It's new, and I've wanted to try it for ages."

"We'll go there then. I love Italian food."

"It's popular. We'll have to book."

"No prob. What's the name of the place? I'll take care of it."

"Mario's," Grace said. "It's on Taka Street."

"If we can't get a booking, do you want to go to the Indian restaurant?"

"I haven't been there for ages. Jeff didn't like spicy food."

Prick. There seemed to be dozens of things Jeff hadn't liked or wanted to do with Grace. Cullen didn't voice his thoughts. He merely raised a hand in farewell and left.

After texting Grace with the details, he booked a table for seven o'clock and spent the rest of the afternoon prepping his lounge for painting.

While he dragged furniture to another room and took down pictures, Grace filled his mind. A dinner date with her was the first step, but he needed to move fast to persuade her to accept him before he had to return to his unit.

If he wanted to win Grace, he had to act now.

His mind wandered as he started stripping the old floral paper from the walls. What would Grace do about the honeymoon? She should go on her trip, but her going alone wasn't ideal.

A bolt of lightning hit without warning.

Grace would've booked for two. Was there any reason

Cullen couldn't take Scumbag's place? The trip would mean an internal flight—to Invercargill, probably. The airline never asked for identification during an internal flight, and the accommodation wouldn't care. They'd received their money. Cullen pondered every angle and couldn't see a downside.

He grinned, liking the idea of stepping into the dick's shoes.

A trip with Grace would allow him to show her how great they could be together, while the jerk-idiot who'd done the dirty on Grace couldn't get to her and persuade her this was all a colossal mistake. Not that Cullen thought Grace would give the cheater another chance.

Even better, the change in scenery might help Cullen too. Last night, he'd slept well, thanks to having Grace at his side. No nightmares. A significant side benefit.

At six, Cullen stopped work to have a shower. He tamed his unruly beard before dressing in black trousers and a cotton shirt. Cullen was glad he had taken the trouble when he collected Grace. She wore a navy-blue sundress covered with bright yellow sunflowers. Her hair was loose, but she'd pulled a few strands back from her face with a clip.

"You look beautiful."

"Thank you. You trimmed your beard this morning. I forgot to mention that I like it."

"Good to hear," he said. Her startled expression told him *the tool* hadn't been big on compliments. *Moron.* "Are you ready to go?"

"Yes." She locked the door without his prompting, and

that made him happy. The last thing he wished for was that idiot pushing his way back into Grace's life. After helping her into the passenger side of his vehicle, he jumped in and backed out of the driveway.

"Did the loser collect his gear?"

"No, but a few of the locals have helped themselves. Word must've spread because I spotted two guys arguing over one of Jeff's leather jackets. It was his favorite." She winged a sly glance in Cullen's direction. "I'm not positive it'll be in one piece after the tugging match they were having."

Cullen chuckled as he pulled into traffic. "At least you're rid of the asshole now."

"Yes, but that doesn't stop the sense of betrayal. I'm focusing on the glass-half-full approach. Luckily, I discovered he's a cheater before we tied the knot and our lives became even more entwined."

Cullen wanted to cheer, but he restrained himself with a nod. "Do you want to know where we're having dinner?"

"I'm hoping you booked at the Italian place because I'm curious about the menu, but if it's Indian, I'll enjoy that too. Nav likes to try out new dishes on me."

Cullen merely nodded again but was glad he'd made reservations at the Italian restaurant for dinner. His hands tightened briefly on the steering wheel, his thoughts rueful. Nav loved his wife. Cullen's jealousy wasn't logical.

Five minutes later, Cullen pulled up in the tiny car park behind the Italian restaurant. He laughed when Grace rubbed her hands together, a devilish grin curling her lips.

"I'll pry any secrets out of the chef in no time," she said.

His risotto and Florentine T-bone steak were better than he'd imagined, and he could tell the tomato bruschetta, the spaghetti and pesto, and her veal main impressed Grace too. The restaurant was busy with no lull in customers, which meant Grace didn't get her chance to quiz the chef.

"Would you like dessert?"

The smile she'd worn for most of the meal slid away. Her gaze dropped to the menu, and she pushed it away. "No, I don't need anything else."

Cullen studied her expression while concealing his strident and pissed thoughts. "I'm having dessert." He scrutinized the menu and picked the taster plate and a chocolate brownie with raspberry coulee because he remembered she adored chocolate of any type. He informed the server of his selection. "Would you like coffee too?"

"Yes, please. Black," she said.

A growl escaped Cullen before he could force it back. The bastard had done a job on Grace and hadn't deserved her. She was a beautiful, sexy, and smart woman who warranted happiness.

He was the man to give her contentment, to help her rekindle her joy, her sparkle.

While they waited for the dessert and coffee, Cullen made his first push. His home renovations could wait. Grace couldn't.

"Have you decided what you're doing about your honeymoon holiday?" Cullen held his breath while he waited for her reply.

She frowned as she met his gaze. "It's my dream trip." Her chin rose, and her mouth set in determination. "I don't see why I should let Jeff ruin this for me."

"Good girl," Cullen said, pride filling him.

"The only thing is I'm not keen on going by myself."

Excellent. The perfect segue to his idea. "I could go with you."

Her mouth dropped open in a perfect round. "You. Go with me?"

Beneath the table, he wrapped his hands into fists while he silently urged himself to keep cool. He forced a shrug. "The flights are internal, and there is no actual security to cause concern. It shouldn't be a problem."

Her brows shot toward her hairline. "But the room is a double."

"Do you trust me?" She shouldn't—not with the acute way he desired her. He'd considered finding a woman to slake his need, but once he'd seen Grace again, the idea held little appeal. "Grace?"

"Of course I trust you. That goes without saying. I'm thinking. Give me a break."

His hands relaxed a fraction as he suppressed a spurt of amusement. He enjoyed Grace's mouthy retorts.

"All right. You can come with me to Stewart Island. Pack walking boots and one smart outfit because there is a place that does a special seasonal menu. I booked months ago because they only have a few tables. Other than that, we'll be fishing, going out after dark to look for kiwis, and hitting the local pub. If that appeals to you, I'd enjoy your company."

Cullen didn't hesitate. "It sounds like my sort of holiday. When do we go?"

"We scheduled the wedding for Friday and were leaving on Saturday."

"It won't take me long to pack," Cullen promised. "I'll do it tomorrow. Do I need to do anything else for the trip?"

"No, I've organized everything, including the airport parking. It's all prepaid."

"We can take my vehicle," Cullen said. "I might bring my camera. I've never seen a kiwi in the wild. We've heard them call in places where we've trained and seen footprints the next morning, but that's as close as I've managed." While he wouldn't push Grace, he wanted her big time, and he wasn't above a little seduction.

She wouldn't know what had hit her by the time he finished.

The desserts arrived, and the waitress hesitated before setting down the plates.

"We're sharing," Cullen said with a smile.

"Right. Why don't I bring spare plates for you?"

"Please," Cullen said.

"I didn't want dessert. I've eaten enough tonight." She groaned. "That pesto pasta was to die for, and it will go straight to my hips. It's an occupational hazard. I need to watch my weight. Jeff said—"

Cullen squeezed her hand. He ignored the zap of awareness, the softness of her skin, and focused on Grace. "This is the last time I'm going to say this because there is nothing worse than a woman going on about her weight. Not everyone is the same build, and we deal with what we get. You are not fat. If that loser you were engaged to thought you were overweight, that is his problem. Not yours."

Grace stared at him with her big green eyes, her pink lips parted.

"Grace?"

"Yes," she whispered.

"If I hear you say you're fat again, there will be consequences."

"Like what?"

Cullen tapped his nose. "You'll find out. Believe me, Grace. You're not overweight. You're stunning and have an old-time movie star figure full of curves. It's attractive. You're gorgeous, and if you'd stop stressing, you'd see I'm right. I'm not the only man who appreciates a woman with curves."

He watched her, focusing on her reaction, prepared to say more to make sure she understood. Her eyes grew round again, and she parted those luscious lips of hers. An attractive pink bloomed in her cheeks.

Tonight, she wore makeup, but she'd kept it light enough for him to discern the freckles across the bridge of her nose. Hell, the men in this suburb must be as blind as the old dog he'd had as a kid if they didn't see her exceptional qualities.

"Which dessert would you like to try first?" he asked when she remained silent. He liked her this way, too—soft and glowing and full of wonder. It reminded him of sex. And just like that, tension snapped down his body, darting from his chest to his groin. He smothered a groan and stared at the desserts on the taster plate. "How about the lemon tart?"

She nodded.

Cullen broke a bit of the tart off with his spoon and held the morsel to her lips. His heart raced as she closed her mouth around the offering. She pulled back, her eyelids dipping a fraction as she cataloged the tart's flavors, her baker's brain analyzing every ingredient. Watching her with food thrilled him because her passion shone through. Her throat worked as she swallowed.

"That is the best lemon tart I've ever tasted. The pastry is crisp and light, while the lemon filling is the perfect blend of sharp and sweet. I can't wait to try the chocolate brownie now."

"My evil plan is working."

Grace rolled her eyes and reached for the brownie.

He edged it out of her reach. "Oh no, you don't. I want to have some brownie first. Give me a chance to place my verdict. See if my opinion matches yours. I've learned a thing or two about food over the years."

She giggled. "I used to try out my different muffin flavors when I was babysitting you."

"You did." And he had fond memories of those times. He scooped up a corner of the brownie and placed it in his mouth. He nodded as he tasted the notes of bitter chocolate and savored the combo of the crispy edge and gooey center. "This will meet your approval too, although it's rich."

He offered a spoonful to Grace. She issued a faint hum of appreciation, and Cullen almost moaned himself. Lord, she did it for him.

"You're right," she murmured and reached for a spoon. "I need more of that brownie to make an informed opinion."

"Huh!" Cullen said, waving his spoon in the air and pulling the brownie out of her reach at the same time.

"Stop teasing me." She tried to sound stroppy, but her breath emerged on a husky note. A suggestion of sexiness that pushed him to imagine the sounds she made during lovemaking. Arousal shot through his body, and he became fiercely glad of the crisp, white tablecloth that hid his lap.

Cullen drew in a hasty breath and forced himself to calm the hell down. His lack of control galled because he was always steady. Disciplined. It was his thing and a strength in his soldiering.

"Cullen? Where did you go? You got a weird expression as if you'd smelled something nasty. I thought the brownie was delicious?"

He cleared his throat. "It is a winner." With willpower, he pushed aside his reaction and the accompanying confusion. He scooped up a bite of brownie along with whipped cream and held it out to Grace. When she went to accept the spoon from him, he shook his head. "No," he whispered hoarsely and waited for her to open her mouth.

Delicate color spread from her cheeks and down her neck, but she didn't take her gaze from his as she accepted the tidbit. Once again, she savored the dessert, and he watched her analyze the tastes and texture.

"You're right," she announced. "The brownie is

exquisite. Which one is next?"

She and Cullen worked their way through chocolate mousse, tiramisu, crème brûlée, and finally chocolate-dipped strawberries along with sips of strong black coffee.

"That was delicious. Thank you for ordering the dessert. I wonder if I can speak with the chef."

"By the looks of it, they're still swamped. Despite the late hour, people are still coming in for dinner. Why don't we grab a business card on the way out? You could give the chef a call once we get back from Stewart Island."

"You're right," Grace said. "They probably want our table. I can see why this place is so popular. I couldn't fault a single thing. The food is excellent, the decor perfect, and the service is top-notch."

"Why don't you thank them by writing a review? Do you still have the blog you started during your *Best Baker* stint?"

"I do, but I've been slack about adding posts. Jeff didn't—" She broke off with a frown. "Come to think of it, Jeff had quite a bit to say about my interests and hobbies, although he did it with dollops of charm. Stupidly, I let him boss me around because relationships are about compromise."

"They are," Cullen agreed. "But one part of a relationship shouldn't need to change everything to please their partner. Not if the change makes little sense, and they can't understand the why. With something like this, letting your partner boss you around is a bad thing. It sets a precedent for the future."

Grace sighed. "All the friends I had in my twenties have married and had children, and we've drifted apart. I'm the last singleton. When Jeff started paying attention, I decided it was my last chance for a family. A mistake. One should never settle. Retrospection is a grand thing."

She wanted kids, and he could picture them since they were his too. A knot formed in Cullen's throat, choking his words. This thing with Grace felt as if it was running out of control, yet he couldn't be sorry. The close call he'd had during his last deployment had changed him, made him consider what he needed to be happy. His mind had gone straight to Grace.

That was sign enough, and spending time with Grace again had only cemented his thoughts into a plan. Now his mission was to seduce the stubborn woman to his way of thinking, and tonight had been an excellent start.

6

CONFRONTATION

DURING THE TRIP HOME, Grace and Cullen discussed the restaurant, their meal, and other easy topics, the vehicle's dim interior leading an intimacy to their journey. A faint edginess assailed Grace. Probably residual annoyance at Jeff and the sense of lingering betrayal.

Cullen indicated a left turn. "My idea is to knock out some internal walls to make the place more open plan. What do you think?"

"I've considered the same thing," Grace said, seizing on the topic. "But I take a while to make important big decisions like that. I mean, what if I didn't like the result? Then, Jeff and I talked. He wanted me to sell and for us to get a more modern place. I won't sell—not now that Jeff has stolen my money." She shrugged. "It's not as if I have time for a major renovation, anyway. My job keeps me busy."

"Well, I don't mind acting the Guinea pig. Our places are mirror images since the same builder constructed them. What the hell?"

Three cars had parked near her and Cullen's driveways. Two men battled for her mattress while Jeff and another man fought over rights to one of his many leather jackets.

Cullen pulled into his driveway, and they exited his vehicle, their gazes on the sidewalk action. The automatic light came on, giving them a much better view.

Grace stared as Jeff screeched at the thin man in jeans and a holey T-shirt who still gripped the jacket with a bulldog tenacity.

"It's mine, you idiot," Jeff shouted. "I didn't throw it out. I have no idea what it's doing out here."

"There's not much of his gear left," Cullen murmured.

The larger of the two men fighting for the mattress got the upper hand and dragged his spoils away. While he struggled to tie it to the roof of his vehicle, the loser stomped to his car and roared off, gunning his engine as he sped down the residential street.

It was then Jeff noticed Grace's arrival. With a Herculean effort, he gained possession of his jacket and stormed in her direction. Grace backed up half a step, relieved when she discovered Cullen's heat at her back.

"You crazy bitch. Why did you throw all my stuff outside? I tried the door, but my key won't work."

"That's because I changed the locks," Grace said sweetly. "You're not welcome in my home."

"We're getting married tomorrow," he snapped.

"Like hell we are," Grace retorted. He was the crazy one,

not her. If he calmly cheated on her now, he'd do it again without a care. That wasn't the life she wanted for herself.

Trust. Respect. *A partnership.*

She'd thought she'd had that with Jeff. Obviously not. He didn't even have the grace to apologize or show remorse for his cheating. This Jeff bore no resemblance to the captivating man from the heady first days and weeks of their relationship. The changes in him had taken place gradually, and she'd failed to notice—until now.

Grace stormed forward two steps and jabbed Jeff in the chest with her forefinger. "I wouldn't marry you if you were the last man on Earth. Where is my money?"

He averted his gaze until she poked him in the chest again.

"You withdrew fifty-five thousand dollars from the joint account. If you don't return it, I'm going to the cops."

"I borrowed it," he said hurriedly.

"You didn't mention it. Don't you think it was manners to at least discuss it with me?"

"Grace, you're being silly. This is a misunderstanding."

She gaped at Jeff for a few seconds, speechless—absolutely speechless—at his effrontery. "A misunderstanding," she mouthed.

Julia hadn't been a figment of her imagination. Their naked bodies in her bed. Fury ripped through her, and she curled her fingers into fists. "I can't believe you. You moron! I refuse to forgive you for fucking the neighbor two days before our wedding!" She punched Jeff in the chest, the force of the blow reverberating up her forearms. Her third punch struck air because Jeff took a backward step. She would've chased him, but Cullen's hands curled around her shoulders, drawing her back.

"That's enough," Cullen murmured in her ear.

Heat filled her cheeks—part anger and part mortification because she'd struck out in a rage. Hitting someone was wrong.

"Do that again," Jeff said with a snarl, "And I'll punch back."

"It's time for you to go," Cullen told him. "What's left of your gear is there. There is nothing remaining in the house. Take your possessions and leave. Grace wants nothing more to do with you."

"Who the fuck are you?" Jeff demanded, temper etched into his round face.

"Grace's friend," Cullen replied.

"You're sleeping with him," Jeff spat. "You have the gall to castigate me—"

"Cullen is my friend. I've known him for years," Grace spat. "Just leave before you make an even bigger idiot of yourself."

"Bitch," Jeff muttered and stomped off to gather up the mess of clothes and possessions littering the footpath. He picked up an empty suitcase and shouted, "You were useless in bed, anyway."

"I am not!" Grace retorted.

Cullen placed a heavy hand on her shoulder and squeezed in a warning. "Don't engage with him. Let's have a nightcap at my place. I don't want you on your own while he's here."

"He wouldn't hurt—" She broke off and considered the

way he'd slept with Julia. He'd threatened that he'd punch her back. He would injure her and think nothing of it.

"Thank you," Grace mumbled.

Cullen curved an arm around her waist and guided her to his front door. After unlocking it, he said, "You go inside and pour us a brandy or a whisky. I have both in the pantry. You know where I keep the glasses. I'll park my vehicle in the garage. I don't want Jeff to get a wild hair and decide to trash my SUV."

"Sure, I'll see you inside." Grace started trembling the moment she stepped indoors. She'd never seen Jeff so angry, with fury making his brown eyes flash. His hands had balled into fists, and she'd made things worse by hitting him. Shame filtered through her because that was so out of character for her.

In the kitchen, she opened the pantry and located Cullen's booze supply. She grabbed the nearest bottle and filled two balloon goblets with a healthy splash of brandy. With a brandy in hand, she claimed a seat in the lounge to wait for Cullen. She kicked off her shoes and wriggled her toes.

The front door opened and closed, and she heard the distinct clunk of the lock engaging. Cullen strode into the lounge seconds later.

"Lots of weird people around tonight," he said, sinking onto the couch beside her.

"Weird like how?" Grace asked with a frown. During the last month, she'd spotted a homeless man wandering along the street, which had been unusual enough to make her stare.

"Like druggies," Cullen said, his tone blunt. "Either that or they were drunk."

"Maybe they heard about the free stuff stacked on the footpath," Grace said, and guilt writhed through her. "I shouldn't have done that."

"If you'd waited for the loser to collect his gear, he might've never budged," Cullen countered. "Don't let it worry you. He messed up, not you." He sipped his brandy. "You should stay here tonight rather than go home. The idiot is still out there, piling his stuff into a vehicle."

Grace rose to go to the window.

"Not with the light on," Cullen warned. "Everyone will see you. Try the kitchen window. You might see what is going on from there."

She heeded the warning to retrace her steps and hover in darkness in the kitchen. Cullen stepped up behind her, and they both peered outside.

"What is he doing?" Grace asked.

"It's hard to say," Cullen said. "It's not the best view from here. Let's get back to our brandy. We've wasted enough time on the idiot today."

"Excellent point." Grace raised her goblet. "To our holiday on Stewart Island."

"To Stewart Island." Cullen shot her a glance. "I know why you picked Stewart Island, but it seems out of character for the loser. Just in the short time I've seen him, he seems more the resort type."

"I thought we weren't talking about Jeff again."

Cullen pulled a face. "Difficult given the circumstances."

"I kept asking Jeff where he wanted to go, but he was busy, so I made an executive decision. To be honest, he didn't gush with enthusiasm when I told him where I'd booked. He's not the outdoor type, but I figured since I paid for the holiday, I should have a greater input."

"Out of interest, what did the moron pay for?"

Grace wrinkled her nose. "Nothing. As I said, he was busy with work and away overseas on business trips. He told me to pay for everything, and we'd sort it out later."

"I bet he did," Cullen muttered. "He's not only paid for nothing, but he's stolen your savings."

Grace scowled. "Put that way, I sound like a real loser."

"Not a loser," Cullen corrected. "You're trusting. You thought he was the man you'd spend the rest of your life with, so why shouldn't you place your faith in him?"

"I feel stupid," Grace muttered.

"He's the wrong man for you," Cullen said. "The right one will be out there somewhere. Just give it time."

Grace snorted. "Easy for you to say. My biological clock is tick, tick, ticking."

"You want children soon?"

"Yes." Rawness shot through her glance. "There's nothing wrong with wanting children, a family."

Cullen smiled, and the tightness in her chest eased. He didn't think she was weird. Jeff had recently informed her he didn't want children, and she was probably too old, anyway. A snort erupted from her. On reflection, there were so many warning signs of their lack of compatibility. She'd swept them aside, thrilled Jeff wanted to marry her. *Idiot.*

"Stop torturing yourself. Everyone makes mistakes or missteps. It makes us human and keeps us humble."

"Yeah? What mistakes have you made?"

Cullen hesitated. "I should've paid better attention at school and tried to get a qualification behind me."

"But you love the army." She got the sense of something else that gave him regrets, but he'd decided not to share. "Didn't you tell me you intended to stay in the army?"

"I do enjoy what I do, but some days the missions are tough, and good people suffer. Administration-types hamper us, and it makes our missions frustrating."

"It's not too late for you to change paths."

"Maybe."

Grace changed the subject. "Have you met the prime minister?"

"I have. I dropped 'round at Josh's place before leaving for my last mission. Ashley was there and had coffee with us. She made blueberry muffins."

Grace's mouth dropped open as she stared at Cullen. "I'm not sure whether you're kidding."

"Not," Cullen said with a grin. He downed the last of his brandy. "Come on. It's getting late, and we have a holiday in our future. You can help me pack tomorrow."

"Do you have something I can sleep in?"

Cullen scanned her up and down, his gaze fast and impersonal. "A T-shirt? Will that work?"

Grace followed Cullen up the stairs and tried not to gawk at his backside too hard. The man was fine, and the woman who won his heart would be so lucky. She shadowed him into his bedroom and came to a halt. Last night she'd been out of it, and this morning, her presence in Cullen's bed had rattled her too much to pay attention to detail. During his last break, he'd renovated, but she hadn't seen the result properly until now.

The single bedroom next to the master was no longer since he'd knocked down the internal wall and combined two into one. He'd also added an en suite bathroom, and the result was lovely.

"Wow, it's beautiful," she said. "I didn't register the changes this morning. Perhaps I can do something—" She came to an abrupt halt because she realized she no longer had a financial cushion.

"Thanks, I'm glad you like it because I turned my spare bedroom into a gym. Tonight will be excellent practice for when we share at Stewart Island."

An explosive noise ripped through the silence that had fallen between them. Cullen strode to the window and glanced outside while Grace squeezed in beside him. The wheels of a car shrieked as they gripped for purchase.

"Was that gunfire?" she asked.

"Yes," Cullen said. "I'll ring the cops. They can deal with this. If someone out there has a gun, we're safer indoors."

He wouldn't get an argument from her.

"I'll grab my phone. I left it downstairs. The towels are in the en suite. If you want to take a shower, go ahead. If I know the cops, this won't be a five-minute phone call." With that, he strode away.

Another shot fired, and Grace winced. Cullen was right. She didn't know what was going on, but some strange people loitered around their suburb tonight.

7

THE HONEYMOON

CULLEN WOKE WITH GRACE in his arms. Obviously a heavy sleeper, Grace was lying on her side and had thrown her leg over his. He could smell her old-fashioned lavender scent and the weight of her breast pressed against his arm. The temptation to kiss her rocked him, but he reluctantly stayed the urge. Grace required time. Once they were alone, sharing a room on Stewart Island, he'd try to show her he cared and perhaps seduce her to his school of thought to make her understand they had possibilities.

A future together.

Or he could go with Plan B—a slightly amended Plan A—and let her become comfortable with the idea of them as a couple. She'd fight him once that amazing brain of hers kicked into gear, and he expected a challenge.

He glanced at his watch. It was six in the morning. He knew from experience he'd never slip into sleep again, so he untangled himself from Grace and left her to rest. After dressing rapidly, he walked down to the kitchen and put on the coffee. Packing wouldn't take long, so perhaps he'd go for a run. Exercise always cleared his mind and helped him see possibilities whenever he encountered a problem.

Deciding to leave the coffee until his return, he grabbed his running shoes from the hall cupboard and pulled them on with quick efficiency. A few minutes later, he jogged down the damp driveway. He dodged a fishy-scented wheely bin on the edge of the curb, the first of many green bins stretching before him, which told him this was rubbish collection day. Summer flowers dipped in their beds, somewhat bedraggled under the weight of the heavy dew.

As Cullen increased his speed, he noted the pair of shoes balanced on the oak tree branch bordering his and Grace's property. He stared up at the scruffy white runners tied together by gray laces. Wasn't this a covert sign for a tinny house? An obscure way of advertising *drugs for sale here*.

His mind clicked into gear, adding clues and skidding to a halt at his conclusion.

Was the dickhead involved in the drug trade?

Cullen recalled everything Grace had told him about her ex-fiancé. The longer he pondered the possibility of drugs, the more it seemed to fit. But how to prove the cretin's involvement? The drug angle would undoubtedly explain the strange people in the neighborhood. Cullen headed away from his house at a jog, his mind busily working, prodding at his theory.

If he were right, Grace's eviction of the creep would

heap problems on the man's head.

Cullen ran for five miles before he turned back toward his house. He arrived to find a silver sedan idling at the curb. A skinny white man in an oversized black hoodie thumped on Grace's door, and when no one replied, he stomped back to the car.

Cullen stopped by the vehicle but continued to jog on the spot. "The owner isn't home," he said. "They've gone out of business. A police raid last night."

"Fuck," the skinny man said. He jumped into the rear of the vehicle, and the driver sped off before he'd even shut the door.

That answered Cullen's question, and he wondered if he should tell Grace. Cullen unlocked the door and let himself inside, striding toward the kitchen. The scent of coffee filled the air, and after guzzling two glasses of water, he poured himself a cup. He had to tell Grace.

Cullen poured a second cup, added a little milk, and carried it up the stairs to his bedroom. He paused in the doorway, enjoying the sight of Grace still asleep, her strawberry blonde hair strewn across his pillow. Deciding not to wake her, Cullen set the coffee on the nightstand and grabbed a bag from the wardrobe. He could start packing without making too much noise.

Grace still hadn't stirred by the time he'd finished. He ran through his mental list and decided he had everything apart from his camera downstairs. The battery needed charging. He retreated to take care of that, poured another coffee, and sat down to read the paper online.

Stewart Island jumped to the fore when he spotted

a travel article detailing the pleasures of a visit. Kiwis. Hunting. Tramping. Fishing. These were among the myriad activities available. He made a note of the bush tucker walk. Grace would love that. Uncertain of Grace's full itinerary, he noted the phone number and their location in the Oban township.

Cullen heard the shower and stood to brew another pot of coffee.

"Morning," Grace said half an hour later. She hovered in the doorway, a faint pink flush in her cheeks.

Cullen wanted to smile, wanted to go to her and wrap her in his arms. Protect her. He did none of these things, instead rose from his stool at the breakfast bar. "Coffee?"

"Please. It's almost eleven. You should've woken me." She approached and perched on the second stool near him.

Cullen reached into the cupboard for a clean mug. "You had a rough day. I figured you could do with the extra rest."

"It took me a while to get to sleep," she confessed. "I'm glad I'm leaving town and won't have to face Jeff's dramatics."

"Talking about Dickhead," Cullen said. "I went for a run earlier this morning. A guy was loitering near your place. A car parked outside your house."

Grace shook her head. "I've noticed a few strangers around. They stick out in our street since it's a cul-de-sac."

Yeah. Cullen agreed, which made his conclusion a bit out-there. Why would the numbskull risk easy detection in an established neighborhood? Unless he was too stupid to realize selling drugs in a family suburb like this asked for trouble. The residents noticed anything out of the ordinary. They spotted strangers. They were the type who policed their area and contacted the cops under suspicious circumstances.

"The guy was looking for your ex and left when I told him the police had raided here last night."

Grace's expression grew slack as she gaped at him. "Why would you tell him that?"

"Because there is a pair of white shoes hanging in the oak tree straddling our property boundaries. That's like a signpost for those searching for a tinny house."

Grace raised her eyebrows. "A tinny house that sells drugs?"

"Yep."

"But Jeff doesn't take drugs."

"Are you sure? Do you know where he lived before he moved in with you? You told me he was away a lot."

"A place in Papatoetoe. He shared it with two other guys. It's why he told me it thrilled him to move into a nice place in a decent area. Their neighbor wore gang colors, and he'd have lots of people around at all hours of the day and night. Sometimes they'd have parties that turned into fights, and the cops would arrive. Jeff told me the street name, but I can't remember right now. It will come to me." She tapped her hands on the counter and sent him a worried look. "It bothers me that Jeff might've been into drugs."

"It's a working theory," Cullen said. "It's probably an excellent idea you're away for a week. Give time for the dust to settle."

"Should we mention this to our other neighbors? To the

cops?" Grace asked.

"No proof."

Grace's scowl dug into her forehead. "I guess we need to wait and see if anything happens, although I can't believe Jeff..." She shook her head. "Surely, I would've noticed drugs."

"Not necessarily. As for watching events unfold, we won't be here," Cullen pointed out.

Grace frowned. "Why don't we mention our concerns to Chris at number twelve? He won't mind monitoring our places since they'll both be vacant. We don't need to mention drugs. We can tell him we're away for a week, and Jeff is being an arse. Both accurate statements."

Cullen considered this before taking a sip of coffee. "Works for me."

THEIR FLIGHT TO INVERCARGILL took just over two hours. After they collected their luggage, they waited for the next leg of their journey—the short fifteen-minute hop to Oban in Stewart Island.

"How come you didn't take the ferry over?" Cullen asked as they strapped into the small six-person plane.

"Jeff gets seasick, and the Foveaux Strait crossing can be fairly hair-raising. I didn't tell Jeff the flight can be as bad as the ferry." She glanced out of a small window. "Looks as if we'll have excellent views given the sunshine." She turned to grin at him. "I'm so excited."

Cullen smiled back. He had a strong stomach, and

seasickness or airsickness didn't bother him. "I remember the sea crossing from when I was a wee lad. We had a family holiday over here for a week."

"Oh, you should've said," Grace murmured. "The last thing I want is for you to feel bored."

"I wouldn't have offered if I didn't want to come. I was five, so the only thing I remember is the bumpy sea, the gigantic waves, and my mother puking. A lot." He wrinkled his nose. "It was disgusting, but she exploded like a fountain."

Grave gave a disbelieving laugh as the pilot taxied the plane onto the runway. "I'm sure she likes the reminder of your Stewart Island holiday."

"That story makes the rounds at family get-togethers. My brother and I like to reminisce with her."

Cullen clasped her hand and pressed closer to peer out of her window. The plane rose until the airport, and the city of Invercargill resembled miniature dioramas. The buildings huddled together in the city center before giving way to a patchwork of paddocks in varying colors of green or brown. Next was the sea and the Foveaux Strait, which separated the South Island and Stewart Island. Today, it was a flat and vivid blue-green with minimal whitecaps to mar its surface.

"How is your brother? I haven't seen him for years. The last time..." She trailed off with a moue of distress.

"My grandmother's funeral. Grace, while I loved my grandmother and miss her, you don't have to tiptoe around the fact."

"Noted. Oh, look. There it is. The island looks so green.

I can't wait to walk in the bush."

Five minutes later, the plane landed on a strip set among more trees. It was a quick hop to their accommodation where Marie and Susan, the owners, allocated rooms and keys.

The Stewart Lodge sat atop a hill. It was a long, flat building with a deck in front that took advantage of the gorgeous view over Oban township and Halfmoon Bay. Tui and fat wood pigeons flitted from tree to tree and let out raucous calls as they chased other birds that got too close.

Their room was one of the five with direct access to the deck and incredible views.

"Breakfast is from seven until nine each morning, and you're welcome to use the kitchen. All we ask is that you clean up after yourself," Susan, a dark-haired woman, said with a bright smile.

"It's even better than I imagined," Grace said to Marie, a blue-eyed blonde. "Thank you."

Cullen noticed Grace glance at the king-size bed dominating the space and frown. He hid his smile. This situation was perfect for his plan, and he intended to try everything in his bag of seduction tricks to get Grace to think of him romantically.

Grace dragged her gaze from the bed. It looked soft and inviting, and the faux kiwi-feather rug gave the bed a luxurious air, as did the multitude of pillows.

"What would you like to do first?" Cullen asked.

"I'd like to unpack and go for a walk to the town. Maybe

have a drink at the pub and book a table for dinner there? I understand it's a busy place this week, and we'll need a reservation."

"Works for me," Cullen said. "What side of the bed do you want? Same as last night?"

Grace's head bobbed up and down when she found it difficult to speak due to mouth dryness. She'd woken during the night to find herself clinging like a passionfruit vine to Cullen. Grace had untangled herself, but when Cullen had woken, she'd been all over him again. She hadn't liked to admit she was awake, too embarrassed by her forward behavior, even if it had been unconscious.

Cullen hadn't mentioned her lapse, though, much to her relief. But it worried her. What if she did it again? Already, she was conscious of his virility, his strength, and his sexy grin. She did not need to spoil their friendship by getting a silly girlish crush.

Cullen cocked his head, humor gleaming in his blue eyes. "Grace? Hello, Grace. Where did you go?"

She shook herself and prayed she wouldn't blush. Unfortunately, her cheeks turned hot straightaway. "Same as last night is fine," she blurted. "Are you okay with the plan to go exploring?"

"Yep. I found something you might like to do during a free afternoon or morning," he said. "Which days do we have things booked?"

"Tomorrow, we have a bus tour in the morning. It can't be an extensive tour because the island has only thirty-two kilometers of roading. We're going fishing for blue cod in the afternoon. The next night we're going out looking for kiwi, and the following afternoon, we have a walk on Ulva Island, a native bird sanctuary. I booked dinner at the special restaurant on the same day as the Ulva Island walk. The rest of the time we can go walking or swimming if the weather is fine. There's also a jet boat ride up a river to a walking hut that looked fun. I think it's the start of one of the week-long walks."

"Perfect. Have you ever seen a kiwi?"

"No," Grace said. "I'm excited at the thought of spotting one and maybe getting a photo."

Ten minutes later, they were on their way.

"I can't believe how steep this hill is," Grace said. "I'm not looking forward to the return journey."

"Lucky for you, you have a powerful soldier to carry you," Cullen murmured.

The idea of his hands on her body had her shuddering. *Not for you, Grace. Friend, remember?* She changed the subject. "Is there anything you want to do while we're here?"

"I wouldn't mind exploring some of the nature tracks. If there is a supermarket, maybe we could pack a picnic lunch."

"Yes! I like that idea."

Their accommodation was at the end of the bay, and they followed the beach around, walking past the primary school, the Kai Kart, which according to Grace's research, sold burgers and fish and chips. They stopped outside the pub.

"Want a drink?" Cullen asked.

"Sure. I'll book the table for dinner. Around seven, okay

for you?"

Cullen nodded. "Want wine or beer or something else?"

"A glass of wine," Grace said and grinned at him. "White, please. Might as well live dangerously."

They entered the pub together and parted ways just inside, with Cullen going left to enter the bar while she walked right into the restaurant to book dinner. She ended up booking dinner for eight but figured the later hour didn't matter. They were on holiday and could sleep later than usual if they got tired.

With all that was going on in her life at present, she could do with more sleep. An afternoon snooze. *A nana nap.* Grace pulled a face. Perhaps not with Cullen around. She wandered into the bar to discover Cullen chatting with the attractive blonde barmaid.

Grace muttered under her breath and stepped up to join Cullen, her fists clenched at her sides. A burning sensation filled her chest—one Grace had no clue what to do with—considering she didn't know where this possessive emotion was coming from. Gah! What was wrong with her today? Why had her thoughts suddenly turned toward Cullen in the romantic sense?

It was Jeff's fault. Obviously. His rejection of her—well, not really rejection, but the way he'd taken another woman to bed had screwed with Grace's mind, hence the weird behavior on her part.

"Did you get a reservation? Michelle says they've been busy this week."

"Eight o'clock," Grace said and forced herself to smile pleasantly at Michelle, the barmaid. "You have a magnificent view from your workplace."

"That we do," Michelle said with an amiable smile. "I hope you enjoy your holiday." She moved away to pour an older man two handles of lager.

"Want to sit outside in the sun?" Cullen asked.

"Yes, that sounds lovely."

Cullen led the way out of the bar, opening the door for her. They sat at one of the wooden tables with a red-and-white umbrella shading them. Grace sat with a happy sigh, the view of the gentle waves rolling onto the sandy shore relaxing her. Two seabirds fought over a tidbit near the waterline while closer to her and Cullen, a redheaded man observed his two young children constructing sandcastles.

Grace sipped her wine—a tart sauvignon blanc. She glanced to her left and spied a supermarket. "Since we're not having dinner until eight, why don't we grab a few beers, a bottle of wine, and a few snacks to have beforehand? We can sit on the deck outside and relax before dinner."

"Great idea," Cullen agreed, turning his face to the sun. "We'll have a wander first and visit the supermarket last."

"Thanks for coming with me," Grace said.

Cullen grinned, and his beautiful face made her heart beat faster. "Hell, it's me who needs to thank you for letting me tag along. I'd be working on the house instead of kicking back and drinking a beer with a beautiful woman. It's great to relax for the first time since I arrived home."

"You're going back," Grace said.

"Yes." Cullen didn't add an explanation, and she didn't

ask for one.

Instead, she changed the subject yet again. "I can't get my head around Jeff dealing drugs from my house."

"Yeah, gut instinct tells me he was into something shady—judging by the visitors you've had to your place and the gunfire last night. Hopefully, the culprits will move on soon, especially if the police are paying attention."

Grace shuddered. "I can't believe I misjudged Jeff so badly, and I'm furious about him stealing my money." Her free hand curled into a tight fist. "I wish I could get my money back, but I got the impression he didn't have it anymore."

"He might've spent it on drugs to resell."

"If he is involved in drugs, that means his overseas trips were drug-related too. As far as I know, he's an accountant, but what if he lied? Everything he told me is suspect now." Tears formed in her eyes as she said that, the stupidity she felt at trusting him overwhelming her.

Cullen set down his beer and reached over to wipe a tear away as it rolled down her cheek. "You might still get your money back. Don't lose hope yet."

"How? I stupidly gave Jeff signing authority on the account. He told me he intended to pay his share into the account the next day." She sniffed and released a forceful breath. "I'm obviously thick. Stupid for trusting him."

Cullen reached for her hand. He curled their fingers together and stared at her. She sensed this scrutiny, even though Grace kept her gaze downward.

"Grace, look at me," Cullen said in a deep voice.

When she didn't obey, he used a forefinger to raise her chin. His gaze was intense and bored right into her. She was certain he glimpsed her fragility, the disbelief that Jeff would do this to her. Her hurt. Her rage.

"Let's make a deal," he suggested.

"What sort of deal?"

"We both agree not to mention the toerag again, and certainly not while we're having fun on Stewart Island."

Grace dragged in a harsh breath and released it on a long exhalation. This time she met Cullen's gaze directly. "All right. I agree. Not one mention of Jeff. He is my past, and that is where I must consign him."

8

RELAXING HOLIDAY

Cullen relaxed fully for the first time in months, this sleepy hamlet the polar opposite of the barren desert region where he'd lived and soldiered only three weeks ago. Color snared his attention in every direction he glanced. The vibrant greens of the native trees and ferns. The turquoise-blue sea. The red-and-white umbrellas shading them from the sun. The white sand and the two toddlers shoveling sand into yellow plastic buckets. Even the scents soothed him: the sea air, the rich aroma of coffee wafting from the restaurant, along with enticing food smells. Fish and chips, if he wasn't mistaken.

His attention turned to Grace, and her warm smile, as their gazes connected, twisted yearning in him. Not something he was ready to admit or embrace, but he was aware of the emotion simmering within him—the longing for roots. Security.

Uncomfortable with the direction of his thoughts, he swallowed the last of his beer and stood. "Another drink, or do you want to wander now?"

"Walk," Grace said.

Cullen held out his hand to Grace to help her stand. She hesitated, but he maintained his patience and waited for her to touch him. A long second later, after she'd raked him with her gaze, she placed her hand in his. She gasped at the first contact, but Cullen didn't let her retreat. Instead, he went for distraction.

"You have callused hands."

"Occupational hazard," Grace muttered, now standing at his side. She furtively tugged to get him to release her.

"I'm frightened," Cullen said. "Please hold my hand until the fear passes."

An inelegant snort escaped her. "You're a soldier. Nothing scares you."

"Not true," Cullen said. "I fear the vehicle I'm in will hit an IED—improvised explosive device," he explained, "or that a sniper will get in a lucky shot, and I'll never see you again." Cullen wondered if he'd gone too far when she frowned at him.

"Me?"

"We're friends, aren't we?"

"Yes," she said without hesitation.

"We pretended to be married at the lodge where we're staying," he added.

"I loathe lying."

"And yet you didn't correct the lady."

"Having to make the explanation is worse. I come off

like a loser, and people feel sorry for me. It was bad enough explaining to the wedding vendors I had to cancel."

"Which is a roundabout way of me telling you that fake husbands and wives hold hands and take the physical contact in their stride," Cullen finished on a triumphant note.

"*Humph!*" Grace said. "Let's check out the shops and the museum before we hit the grocery store."

They wandered down a side street and passed a café and one or two tour operators before Cullen spotted the one he wanted. "How would you like to do a Nature's Pantry tour?" he asked. "It's a three and a half-hour walk through the bush where they show you native plants, which are great for medicinal or culinary purposes."

"I saw this tour, but J—the person who was to come with me hates walking."

"It sounds like fun to me," Cullen said. "Let's see if we can fit a tour into our schedule."

They could, and after paying and getting their tickets, Grace pointed out the museum. "It's brand new and recently opened after they grew out of the old one."

"Why don't we save that for later in the week? In case we have a rainy day," Cullen suggested.

Nobody could call the township of Oban large. Cullen retook possession of Grace's hand, and they wandered onward past a shop selling clothing made of merino wool. They weren't far from the jetty now, where the ferries disgorged their passengers.

"That's where we catch the boat for blue cod fishing," Grace said.

"Looking forward to that. I can't recall the last time I went fishing. Ready to hit the supermarket? It looks as if we've covered most of the town."

Grace smiled. "I like that it's not big."

In the supermarket, Cullen took custody of a green shopping basket. The aisles weren't wide, so to his regret, he had to release her hand.

She scurried ahead, choosing items to place in their basket. Crackers. Cheese. A carton of dip. Crisps. A packet of sweet biscuits. Two bottles of wine and a six-pack of beer. Grace hesitated when they reached the confectionery shelf.

"Which one is your favorite?" Cullen asked.

Grace sighed. "Whittaker's chocolate. I'm a patriotic New Zealander at heart, so I adore their products. No, I won't get chocolate. I've been eating enough lately."

"Your favorite?" Cullen reached for a bar of plain milk chocolate and chucked it into the basket. "I haven't had chocolate for ages."

"Berry and biscuit," she blurted.

Cullen grabbed one and placed that in their shopping basket too. "We're going to be busy with lots of outdoor activities. It might be nice to have an energy boost."

At the checkout, Grace argued about who was paying.

"Cupcake," Cullen said and pressed a quick kiss to the tip of her nose. He almost laughed when he noted the widening of her pretty green eyes. The blaze of shock at the intimate caress. "Now that we're married, we don't need to argue over who is paying for what."

While she was doing a creditable goldfish impression,

Cullen pulled his wallet from his pocket and placed four twenties on the counter.

"Put the change in the charity tin," Cullen said, gesturing at the small sign beside the till.

"Thanks," the male checkout operator said with a smile.

Grace unfurled the shopping bag she'd placed in her pocket and quickly packed their groceries.

"Let me carry that," Cullen said.

Grace gave the checkout man a rueful smile. "We'd better buy one of your bags. The wine and beer will be heavy."

"Brilliant plan," Cullen said. "I'll carry those. I bet you've forgotten the hill we have to climb before we get back to the lodge."

Grace groaned. "Point taken. I'll work that chocolate off with no trouble walking up and down that peak several times a day."

Cullen was used to lugging equipment and belongings up mountains, but Grace's face turned bright red, and her breaths came in hoarse pants before they reached the top.

She staggered into their room, and after dropping her bag of shopping on the floor, she fell onto the bed.

"I assumed I was reasonably fit since I'm on my feet for hours each day. I was wrong," she said with a gasp. She rolled over onto her back and glared up at him. "Don't laugh. You're not even breathing hard. For you, it was an easy stroll down the road."

Cullen chuckled at the accusation.

"I said don't laugh. If I've got sore muscles, I won't be much fun tomorrow."

"You can soak in the bath, and I'll give you a massage. You'll be fine."

Grace got a peculiar expression on her face, intriguing Cullen and prodding at his curiosity. "Where did your mind go?"

"Um..." She bit her bottom lip, drawing Cullen's avid attention.

"Grace?"

"I was imagining your hands on me," she murmured. "Wondering how rough your calluses would feel against my skin."

He cocked his head, sensual awareness throbbing to life in him. "You like that idea."

She groaned and closed her eyes. "My brain is faulty. You're younger than me, but I keep forgetting that. Now change the subject before I embarrass myself any further. If I don't shut up, you'll be sorry you ever agreed to this farce."

"I'm having fun," Cullen said, which was nothing less than the truth. "Do you want me to run the bath for you?"

"Yes," she said. "That would be lovely."

Cullen wandered away but didn't let himself smile until his back was to her. Little did Grace know, but he had her in his sights, and if he had his way, there'd be loads of touching and intimacy. This was a great start to their honeymoon—the best.

He discovered a jar of bath crystals in the bathroom and added a generous handful to the water. They frothed into fragrant bubbles immediately, a light floral scent flooding the bathroom. With the water still running, he returned to

Grace.

"Do you want a glass of bubbles while you're soaking?"

"We didn't buy any."

"I packed a bottle in my bag," he said. "I put it in the fridge while you were unpacking."

"That was sneaky. Bubbles sounds lovely."

"Get in your bath, and I'll bring it in for you."

She stared at him for a long moment but finally shrugged. Cullen grinned again. It wouldn't hurt if she let loose and got tiddly.

He gave her a few minutes before he opened the champagne and poured a glass. "Grace, are you in the bath?"

"Yes." Grace's voice sounded muffled.

"I'm coming in," he said, tapping the door and opening it at the same time.

Grace sat in the tub with bubbles up to her neck when he walked into the bathroom. He smiled, enjoying this intimate moment. The first of many, he hoped. He handed over the wineglass.

"Sorry about the glass, but our room didn't come equipped with flutes," he said.

Grace sighed. "Thank you. This is so decadent. I never have time for this sort of relaxation. Work is busy, and then there was the wedding plans and organization."

Cullen bent over to place his finger across her lips. Her eyes flared with shock, and he fought back a smile. "No mentioning the wedding or the J-word. Okay?" He lifted his digit a fraction.

"Sorry, it slipped out. The champagne is delicious. I

don't have it often."

"Enjoy and take your time. I'm going to sit outside and enjoy the view with a beer. Come and join me when you're ready." He started to leave and paused. "Would you like music?"

"I don't listen to music often either. That sounds perfect."

He nodded. "Won't be a sec." He returned in seconds with his phone and chose a quiet playlist. A ballad poured out, and they shared a smile.

"Thank you, Cullen."

"No problem, cupcake." He left then, grabbed a beer, and settled outside. The late afternoon sun still held warmth, so he whipped off his shirt. Grace had done well choosing the accommodation. This view over Oban and the sea was stunning. He rose to grab his camera and returned to take a couple of photos. After the desert climate where he'd spent the last few months, this was paradise, and he intended to take advantage of every minute.

A pair of tuis squawked at each other in noisy protest, the territorial birds flapping their wings and chasing each other from tree to tree. One of the blacky-brown birds, with their distinctive tuft of white throat feathers, gave way and fled to find a more peaceful haven.

Beyond, in the township and the bay, people and boats arrived and departed. This was a view he could watch for days without becoming bored. He sipped his beer and pondered his next move with Grace, highly satisfied with his progress. This holiday was the best thing to happen to him. Grace, too. He'd needed a sense of purpose, and now all he had to do was capitalize on this opportunity.

Jeff stomped into the dingy motel unit and chucked what remained of his possessions on one of the two single beds. The bitch! What the hell had she been thinking? Tossing his stuff out of the house without a by-your-leave. And the way she'd marched into the bedroom and sprayed that crap on him and Julia. Surely, she realized he was a man with needs?

Grace had suited his purposes because she worked a job that kept her busy. Even better, she'd had a financial cushion. That she'd been rubbish in bed hadn't bothered him. He'd fucked her once a week and continued hooking up with his current lady friends. He stroked his chin and grinned, an image of Julia sucking him off filling his mind. Suction to rival a vacuum cleaner and the way she'd taken him so deep down her throat. Man, he didn't regret bedding Julia for one moment.

His grin fled as Grace slipped back into his mind.

The bitch.

Because of her, he had his associates on his tail, and if they caught him, he didn't fancy his chances of escaping with his life. It was Grace's bloody fault for placing him in this position, and he would not let her get away with kicking him out of her home.

He'd had a good thing going with Grace, and he refused to let her screw up his life.

But what to do?

His statues had disappeared.

With the help of his hidden camera, he'd tracked down most of the people who'd grabbed his gear. He'd retrieved one statue, and he'd approach the man who'd grabbed two more tomorrow. Given the camera angle, it'd proved challenging to work out which two of the four statues they'd taken. One of his four gnomes was still missing.

Three of the four, he didn't care about, but the fourth—if he was to stay alive, he had to get the statue before his boss caught up with him.

Bloody Grace. She'd pay for this bit of treachery.

9

Jeff Reaches Out

"What is your official verdict on the dinner?" Cullen asked, taking in Grace and the rest of the diners in the busy pub restaurant. They stood at the desk, waiting for a waitress so they could pay for their meal. "Good, bad, or indifferent?"

"The blue cod was delicious. It's hard to beat fresh fish. My meal was tasty pub fare. Not terrible, but it won't make my all-time top five meals either."

Cullen nodded at her verdict and reached for her hand once he'd sorted out the check.

Bemused, Grace let him clasp her hand. Outside, it was dark with a dozen streetlamps illuminating the footpath beyond the pub. Cullen tugged her along the waterfront and they left the pub behind. The whoosh of waves relaxed her, and she realized she hadn't felt this contented for months. Cullen's hand was warm in hers, and she was glad he walked at her side. Once they passed the school and the Kai Kart, the streetlamps ended. She'd brought a torch with her but had left it in their room.

"You ready to handle the hill?"

"After the champagne and the wine at the pub, I can do anything." She punctuated this with a giggle. "*I truly can do anything.*"

"You can," Cullen murmured. "Why didn't you get your own place after you finished the contest? What made you decide to return to your job?"

Grace sighed. "I didn't think I was good enough."

Cullen's fingers tightened on hers. "That wasn't what you told me before I left last time."

"Yeah, I know. I started going out with Jeff not long after you left. He talked me into keeping my current job and not spending the money I'd saved." *Oops*, she was breaking the no Jeff rule. She thought Cullen might comment, but he didn't.

"And now you know why," Cullen said.

"Yeah. *Bastard.*"

Cullen laughed. "I haven't heard you swear before."

"I try not to cuss." She hesitated, the pause weighty. She rushed to fill the silence. "I figured it was excellent training for later when I had children." Grace tensed. Bother, she hadn't meant to mention that either.

"I'd like children," Cullen said, surprising the heck out of her.

"You would?"

"Yeah. Before I get too much older. My friends have kids now. Josh and Ash are expecting their first child. Josh told me before you arrived."

"That's wonderful news. I take it that few people know because I haven't heard anything on the news."

"No, they haven't made the public announcement yet," Cullen said. "They're telling friends and family first, although the press constantly speculates about a baby bump."

"I can't believe you're friends with the prime minister's husband." The incline increased, and Grace's breaths started coming faster. It was dark at this end of the town, and Grace's imagination jumped into overdrive. Her fingers tightened around Cullen's.

"I hope that by the end of this holiday, I'll be bounding up this hill like a jackrabbit," she gasped out. "You'd think I'd have reasonable fitness with the amount of walking I do during a day at work." She glared at him in accusation. "You're not even breathing hard."

"We're constantly training, even when we're on leave. It can be a matter of life or death for us, so our fitness is important."

"I know you run, but what else do you do for training?"

"When we're at our base, there's an obstacle course they're constantly changing. We do long runs and hikes up mountains while wearing our packs. We're always doing weapons training and special exercises."

"Such as?" Was that a rustle in the bushes to their right?

"Jumping out of planes, swims in the ocean, scaling buildings. Everything and anything the bosses can use to challenge us and help us work as a team."

"I see. What do you do when you're on holiday? I've

seen you running, but what else?"

"I'm a member of the local gym. Sometimes, I'll go swimming with friends—diving or something like that. Hunting, fishing, or camping. Most soldiers enjoy an outdoor life."

"I can't remember the last time I camped," Grace gasped out, each breath coming in a harsh pant. The rustling had ceased, but she still peered into the darkness, alert to any further noises. "Perhaps I should start a fitness plan."

"The secret is to discover an activity you enjoy. It doesn't have to be a high-power exercise. Keep going. We're past the steepest part of the hill."

An involuntary groan escaped her, but she plodded onward. "I enjoy bushwalking. I love seeing and hearing our native birds and identifying the trees."

"Commit to doing a walk once or twice a month. Keep it as a treat or a pick-me-up if you've had a tough week."

They rounded the bend in the road, and something big bounded in front of them. Grace let out a squeak of fright before she could stop herself and dragged her hand from Cullen's.

"Steady," Cullen said. "It was just a herd of deer feeding in the clearing there. We gave them as big a fright as they gave us."

Grace patted her chest atop her thudding heart. The crashing and drum of hooves continued before trailing off. "It's so dark! I'd prefer to see a kiwi. I might still expire in shock, but it would be a pleasant one."

Cullen laughed. "We might manage that. I was speaking with a local earlier today while you were booking dinner in the restaurant. He told me if we walk to the local rugby field, we have a decent chance of spotting a kiwi. All we need to do is make sure our torch has a red light so we can watch them without upsetting the birds."

As they turned onto the garden path belonging to the lodge, Grace grasped his arm, excitement trumping her fatigue. "Can we do that? Really?"

He laughed again. "Yes, to both questions. I didn't pack a torch, but the lodge owner might have one we can borrow."

"I have a flashlight, but I'll ask tomorrow if we can borrow one for you." Her enthusiasm made the last of the walk—a few stairs that led up to their deck and room—more manageable. "Thank you, Cullen. I've had a lovely day—much better than the earlier part of my week."

"Glad to be of service."

Cullen unlocked their door to the summons of her ringing phone.

"Probably my mother. She thought I should cancel this trip to Stewart Island. I didn't tell her you were coming along because I didn't want a lecture or dozens of questions." Grace fumbled through the handbag she'd left in their room in favor of a smaller, over-the-shoulder bag to find her phone. "Ah!" She plucked it from the bottom of her bag and tapped to accept the call.

"Hello!" Too late, she registered the number was one she didn't recognize.

"Grace," a familiar voice snapped. "Where are you?"

"None of your business," Grace fired back, her pulse rate jumping into a crazy beat. "Why are you calling me?

From the moment I caught you in bed with Julia, our relationship was done."

"Hang up," Cullen said.

"Who is that?"

"None of your business," Grace said, taking pleasure in repeating the words.

"Is that same guy with you?" Jeff demanded.

"Do you think you're the only one who has *friends* of the opposite sex?"

Jeff snorted. "You don't have what it takes to attract another man. You were lucky I was willing to marry you."

Grace increased her grip on her phone, and she jolted upright, tension straightening her shoulders. She got Jeff was trying to needle her. Make her feel small. Heat flushed her body, her anger writhing snakelike through her and poking at the sense of betrayal she'd experienced since discovering him in bed with Julia.

It wasn't going to happen.

Not again.

He didn't get to belittle her or make this Grace's fault.

She was great at her job, and while she bore distinct curves and would never be stick-thin, that didn't mean she wasn't attractive. She'd listened to Cullen when he spoke. He was a handsome and sexy man—one any woman would thrill to have at her side. She grasped on to what Cullen had told her and refused to let his spoken encouragement go unheeded.

Jeff was a jerk, and she didn't need him in her life. She deserved love and support and didn't need to put up with Jeff's crap.

She was worthy.

It was time to remember that and not let Jeff's assertions poison her mind.

"I don't want to talk to you, Jeff. We're not a couple any longer. You're a mere speed-bump in my life. Goodbye." Her finger hovered above the disconnect button before his panicked tone reached her.

"Wait! Grace, what did you do with my gnomes?"

"What?"

"My *hear no evil* statues. I've tracked three of them down, but one is missing."

"Tell someone who cares," Grace said and hung up on him.

"What did the loser want?" Cullen asked.

Guilt flitted through Grace, but she lifted her chin and met Cullen's gaze. "He wants to know the location of his missing statue. Um, I have it. After we discussed them, I took the one flipping the bird because that's what I wanted to do to Jeff."

"You have it here?"

"It's in the bottom of my bag. I intended to put it on display as a reminder of how I felt about Jeff."

Cullen chuckled. "So why didn't you? Why is it still in your suitcase?"

"I chickened out," she confessed.

"I guess Jeff likes the statue. You didn't tell him you had it."

Grace pulled a face. "No, when it comes to that man, I'm not feeling nice."

"Do you want a nightcap? We could have a brandy out

on the deck."

"Sounds great," Grace said. "I'll get the statue to show you."

In the bedroom, she plucked the statue out of her bag. She peered at the ten-inch-tall white gnome with its gold decoration and couldn't see anything different from the other three she'd tossed out with Jeff's belongings.

"What's taking you so long?"

"I'm coming." Grace hustled outside to join Cullen, where he sat on the deck.

The sound of the waves whooshing gently to shore drifted to her while the lights of Oban sparkled like jewels set around the bay. Not a single vehicle rumble interrupted the music of the night, and it was nice not hearing the rev of cars or motorcycles, the chug of buses, and the screech of trucks on the motorway. This place was peaceful and a rest for her senses.

She took a seat opposite Cullen and set the statue on the table.

"Why don't you sit over here?" Cullen suggested, patting the bench right beside him.

Grace's pulse stuttered as she shot him a stare. Cullen was confusing her. He'd held her hand, kissed her, and she had no idea what this meant. Now he wanted her to sit next to him. Their thighs would touch. Their shoulders.

"W-why?"

"Because I enjoy having you near, and I thought we could stargaze together. Maybe listen for a kiwi calling or a morepork."

"All right." Grace nodded and rose again. Something

about Cullen seemed different this time, and she couldn't pinpoint what or why he'd changed. Sometimes, he grew quiet, and she wondered if his last mission was weighing on him. Working in a war zone must be taxing. She found it stressful enough to manage a busy kitchen. She had no clue how he kept returning to his unit, although she'd never say that to him. Grace slipped into the seat beside him, and his arm draped around her shoulders.

"This is better. Do you know any of the constellations?"

"No," Grace said.

"Me neither," Cullen admitted. "Although I'm pretty good at navigating. Lucky for me."

"This is so nice here. Thank you for talking me into coming instead of canceling. If it'd been up to me, I would've stayed at home and moped."

Cullen cupped her cheek and turned her to face him, the faint drag of his finger pushing a shudder through her. She fought her desire to close her eyes and lean into him and instead grabbed her brandy before resettling herself still within touching distance but far enough away to let her breathe.

"I should thank you," he said. "This trip beats stripping wallpaper and sanding any day."

A companionable silence fell between them. Grace sipped her brandy and savored the burn of the liquor on her palate, relaxing against Cullen's side. It was beautiful here, and as she'd told Cullen, she was so glad she'd gone against her initial instincts and proceeded with the trip.

A morepork—New Zealand's native owl—hooted, its mournful cry echoing around them. Almost immediately, another morepork returned the call.

"I wonder why the idiot decided you had the statue?"

Grace shrugged. "Maybe he's clutching at straws and thought he could talk me into taking him back or something stupid like that. Who knows?"

Cullen reached for the statue and lifted it, holding it in the light. He frowned and tapped it with his forefinger. "It's not exactly attractive with that sneer on its face and the raised forefinger," he said finally.

"No," Grace said.

"The part that bothers me is why he's asking you for it. We watched people helping themselves to his possessions. You told me you put the matching statues out on the sidewalk, right?"

"Yes, he told me he tracked them down."

"How, if people took the statues?"

"Perhaps he rang to learn what I'd say."

"Possibly." Cullen studied the statue again. He shook it, listening closely before frowning. "It's ugly."

Grace took the statue from him and set it on the table. "You said we weren't discussing anything from home."

"You're right." Cullen picked up his brandy and finished the last of the liquor. He yawned. "I don't know about you, but I'm tired. It always takes me a while to get back to a normal sleeping pattern."

"I'll be in as soon as I finish drinking my brandy."

"Well, don't do something stupid like try to sleep on the couch. Come to bed. I don't bite. Much." He grinned at her, his smile wide in the dim light.

"Good to know," Grace said dryly. "I guess I'd better

apologize ahead of time for acting like a clinging vine. If I keep you awake, just push me back to my side of the bed."

"I might like a cuddle."

Grace snorted. "You're much younger than me. Why would you want an older woman groping you in the middle of the night?"

"Grace, you're not old. You're gorgeous, have a glorious smile, and your curvy shape does it for me. You remind me of an old-fashioned movie star."

Her mouth opened and closed and opened again. Cullen chuckled and returned to her side. She stared up at him wordlessly when he tapped her chin with his forefinger. Taking the hint, she closed her mouth, and he laughed again.

"You need to learn how to take a compliment."

"I'm not used to them."

"The men who've passed through your life are idiots," he said and walked away, leaving that declaration resounding around her.

She blinked, trying to make sense of his words. He hadn't made a big deal about her eating something other than salad for dinner. Toward the end, Jeff had issued snide remarks, making her self-conscious and tense each time they'd gone out to dinner together. Now she understood Jeff's proposal, and it hadn't been because he'd fallen madly in love with her.

The back of her eyes prickled as memories flickered with Hollywood movie crispness through her mind. At least, she'd learned of his character flaws before their marriage. She had to keep telling herself this was a blessing. She'd found out before her relationship became angry and bitter and even more expensive.

She tipped up the brandy goblet and drank the last mouthful.

Instead of marriage, she was sharing a holiday with a sexy soldier and enjoying every minute. This vacation was much more fun than she would've had with Jeff if she were honest. She collected both empty goblets and carried them inside.

A small alcove with a fridge and tea-making facilities passed as a kitchen, and she set the goblets there to wash in the morning. Cullen appeared, passing her on his way to the bed. She halted, her eyes wide, and to her embarrassment she gaped. While she'd seen him mowing the lawn or running shirtless, this time somehow seemed different. More intimate.

"Something wrong?"

"Yes. No. Of course not," Grace spluttered. "Ah, have you finished in the bathroom?" *Grace, you're acting like an idiot. Cullen saw you sitting in the bath earlier. You had bare shoulders. How is this different?*

"Sure, it's all yours."

Grace took her time, a part of her hoping Cullen had fallen asleep by the time she'd finished. She brushed her teeth, cleaned off her makeup, and then realized she didn't have her nightdress with her.

It was sitting under her pillow, waiting for her to grab it. Nightdress was a vague description. It was more negligee since this was her honeymoon, after all. The wispy red silk left little to the imagination, and she should've remembered this before she left home.

In her defense, she'd packed her bag two weeks ago and had forgotten what she'd put aside to celebrate her wedding. New clothes. Special clothes. Skimpy clothes.

She swallowed hard.

Stuff it.

She was going to wear that negligee.

10

You're The One I Want

WHILE CULLEN LOUNGED IN bed and waited for Grace to bolster her bravery, his mind drifted to the dickhead. He hadn't wanted to waste a second of energy on the cheating bastard, but unfortunately, the moron kept jumping into Grace's honeymoon like a carnival jack-in-the-box. Cullen didn't think Grace had twigged yet, but adding the clues together was ridiculously easy. The stolen money, the constant business trips, the shoes tossed over the tree bordering his and Grace's properties, the shady characters lurking in their neighborhood.

The idiot was hip-deep in the drug world.

From the little Cullen had seen of him, the dipstick didn't strike him as the operation's brains, which meant this situation became a little more serious. Lucky for Grace, she was at the bottom end of the country and away from the drama in Auckland. Cullen decided he'd ask Josh to do some digging if he had time.

He tapped a quick text to his friend, promising to call him later with more details.

Also, in the morning, he needed to inspect that gnome statue more closely. The dumbass had sounded desperate to get it back. Cullen's jaw tightened. It was also possible the douche had installed concealed cameras to aid him in his business. Smart move, but not so great for Grace.

He loathed the idea of the tosser spying on Grace's every move. That showed something deeper and more sinister. The jerk had planned to marry her and continue the pretense. Why? He'd already taken Grace's money, and if he was sleeping with other women, he cared little for her.

It was a wonder the neighbors hadn't reported the strange visitors, but Grace hadn't noted them as odd until this week.

Cullen pondered this anomaly. Perhaps they arrived to a schedule. Most of their neighbors had long driveways with attractive gardens in front. Cullen tapped his chin, the puzzle nagging at him.

His phone beeped in a return text from Josh.

Where are u? I thought you were doing reno at your place. You're not home.

"Nosy bugger," Cullen muttered with a broad grin. He texted back. **I'm on Stewart Island with Grace. Will call tomorrow. Busy.** His smile turned evil as he tapped send and switched off his phone.

Grace scuttled from the direction of the bathroom and sidled around the bed, a flowery sweetness floating in her wake. She opened a drawer without glancing his way, prompting his curiosity. He would've bet good money Grace would've changed in privacy. She shot him a glance and blushed a deep red before she turned away.

"Something wrong, Gracie?"

"N-no," she murmured, the reply so low, he barely heard.

"Your behavior indicates otherwise."

"Shut your eyes," she ordered. "Are they shut?"

"Yes," Cullen lied. He wasn't about to forfeit an opportunity to see any part of his Grace. Usually, she dressed in flowing layers that concealed and did little to showcase her hourglass figure. That had changed this week, and her hesitation now intrigued him. That she might change while in the same room as him had his pulse racing and any gentlemanly behavior squashed. This was his Grace, and he'd waited for so long.

Hell, he'd almost lost out to the knucklehead.

He wanted Grace in his life permanently.

Yeah, this was war.

Grace hesitated, hovering by the side of the large bed. At least, it had seemed massive before Cullen had taken possession of half of the king mattress.

Could she do this?

A sharp, short giggle burst from her. Liquid courage. She noted Cullen's intense interest, and her hands trembled, but she unbuttoned her blouse and shrugged the silky fabric off her shoulders. Instead of picking it up straight away, she let the garment drop to the floor. Her bra was next, and a quick flick of her wrist had her heavy breasts freed from the binding. She let the lacy garment slip to the floor too. She reached for the flimsy red negligee and slipped it over her head. A low masculine groan echoed through the still room, and Grace whirled to face the bed.

"I told you to keep your eyes shut." Accusation shaded her words.

"No, you told me to close them. You didn't mention a time limit." His grin and the expression in his sparkling blue eyes were decidedly wolfish.

His amusement infected her, and she had to force her return scowl. Her stomach did a weird flip—not nausea, but a close nerve-related cousin. "We're friends. You shouldn't stare at me like a wolf. It...it makes me uncomfortable," she finished in a rush.

Cullen stilled, his smile disappearing. "No, we're not friends."

"What?" She didn't have to pretend confusion as a dagger of pain sliced and diced her chest. "If we're not friends, then why are you here? I thought you liked me."

Cullen sat straighter in the bed, a brooding frown settling into his features. His broad chest rose and fell, attracting her attention. *His naked chest.*

When she realized she was staring, she wrenched her gaze off him and aimed it at her feet. Much safer. That way, he couldn't see how much he'd upset her. She'd had a cheerful buzz going when they'd come inside. She'd thought he enjoyed her company as much as she relished his.

"Gracie, look at me."

"My name is Grace."

"All right." Cullen's voice dropped in temperature. "Will you please let me explain?"

Swallowing hard, she lifted her gaze, her heart beating faster and fear blotting out her happiness.

"Why don't you sit on the bed before you topple on your arse?"

She followed this instruction, her pulse racing. Her mouth tasted of chalk and desert dust, and no amount of swallowing helped to moisten the aridness or drag back her feel-good mood.

"Grace, a long time ago, you told me you valued the truth."

Her throat worked in another useless gulp. "I do, but that doesn't mean I'm not apprehensive, that I don't fear what the truth might mean."

Cullen issued a weighty sigh, almost as if she'd disappointed him. "Oh, Grace. Don't you understand? This is the truth. I've had a crush on you for years. At first, I hoped the sentiment would fade because we have six years between us, as you keep reminding me. You didn't think of me in that way, so I kept the banter going and resigned myself to enjoying each moment I spent with you. The last couple of tours have been hard. I've lost friends." It was his turn to swallow. "Close friends. It was you who got me through. I'd read your emails, and they'd place me back at home. You were the one I wanted. The last time I came home, you soothed me. Quiet moments with you helped me to put myself back together again. But you didn't show any signs of change. You still thought of me as a friend. I figured I had time to change your mind."

Grace pressed her hand to her mouth, shocked, surprised, amazed by his confession and unable to formulate anything resembling a reply.

Cullen continued. "This last mission was bad, Grace. I lost another two friends. Brothers. They were family because we lived and worked and had trained together from the beginning. After Chad and Jimmy died, everything changed. I did a lot of soul-searching about what I wanted. You figured in most of my plans, so I made myself a promise. I had a plan until I met you outside your place, and you mentioned you were getting married. It almost killed me, hearing that," he whispered. "I understand you've just come out of a relationship and are feeling hurt and raw. Disillusioned with the male sex, but I wanted you to know the truth—how I feel about you. Why don't you finish undressing and get into bed? That crook in your neck can't be comfortable."

"Okay." Grace stood on shaky legs and wriggled out of her skirt. She took a few moments to pick up her discarded clothes and toss them over the back of an easy chair. It was the same place where Cullen had placed his garments, and she frowned at the combo of clothing. Shaking herself, she hustled to the bed, her skin rippling with a prickle of awareness the entire time while her mind replayed his confession.

Cullen tugged back the covers on her side of the bed. "Your body is gorgeous, and it really does it for me. I've dated other women, and let me tell you, the skinny, diet-conscious ones are a pain in the butt. They suck all the enjoyment from a delicious meal. We eat dozens of MREs—that's meals ready to eat—and they are not a culinary experience. They contain the right vitamins and minerals, but the taste and flavor are elusive. They're convenient. A meal should be a sensual experience. When I share a meal with a woman like you who knows food and luxuriates in the flavors and textures, it makes the lunch or dinner or breakfast way more memorable. An experience. Please remember that."

"But I'm considered overweight."

Cullen shrugged. "Maybe, but you can't fight genetics and your given body shape. All you can do is work with what you've got. Eat balanced meals and exercise."

"You make it sound easy."

"In my experience, if a person wants something badly enough, they'll do the hard work to achieve their goals. If you're losing weight for someone else, then you're going to fail. You're a talented chef and not just at baking cakes and cookies. Own it and don't let anyone drag you down."

Her throat grew tight, emotion backing up behind a knot that swallowing refused to shift. Cullen sounded sincere. He meant every word.

He frowned, his expression neutral while he waited for her response. "Why don't you come closer? You still don't look comfortable over there."

Grace hesitated. The urge to ask questions grew in her, but that stubborn knot remained. Her mouth opened and closed before she pressed her lips together in exasperation. No matter what Cullen said, she considered him a friend, and she trusted him. She shifted her butt until her legs brushed Cullen's longer limbs. He slipped an arm around her shoulders, a pleasant heat sinking into her skin. For an instant, she held herself still, then she relaxed against Cullen.

"Thanks," he murmured and kissed the top of her head.

Her confusion returned and with it disbelief. Cullen truly liked her in that way?

"Stop thinking so hard," he said, his warm breath sending a frisson down her neck and across her chest. The sensation sank to her breasts and signaled her nipples. Grace gulped, embarrassment a hairsbreadth away.

"That's better," he said in a gruff voice. "Now, where was I before we got distracted by food and body image? Oh, yeah. The wedding. That news blindsided me, but I considered it a sign when you came to the pub. I decided I'd do anything to pursue you and win you around to my way of thinking. I care for you, Grace. Hell, I'm more than halfway in love with you. But, as I also said, you've just finished with the moron, and I get that you'll want to go slowly, that's if you're interested in me."

Grace turned her head to check his expression. His eyes glowed in the faint light of the bedside lamp, and what she glimpsed in them was tenderness. "I—"

He placed his fingers over her mouth. "Think about us over the next few days because this has come as a surprise to you. Give yourself a chance to become used to the idea. The six years between us is nothing and not worth the worry."

"Cullen, do you really want to have children?"

The flash of longing in his eyes gave her the answer. He wanted to have kids, so one of them needed to be practical.

"I'm almost thirty-five. You're in your late twenties. I don't even know if I can have children."

"Grace." Cullen's big hands cupped her face and turned her to face him. "Sure, I'd like to have a family, but don't you get it? It's you who matters to me. You're the one I want. My friends have kids, and since my friends are more like brothers, I'm an uncle to dozens of boys and girls already. If I want to spend time with short people, all I have to do is offer to babysit. There are heaps of other options: adopting, fostering kids, or babysitting for my friends. Hell, we could even get a cat or dog or both. You're the important one to me in this equation."

Grace's mouth rounded, but not a scrap of sound emerged.

"What were you going to say?" he finally growled.

"Your declaration has taken me by surprise. So much has happened in the last week, and I feel as if I can't gain my footing."

"Which is why I'm suggesting you think about my proposal."

"You've said a lot," she said. "It's going to take me a while to get my head around it."

"Understandable. We'll just have fun this week. I've almost completed my four-year term of service. This time, I've decided not to sign up again. Josh offered me a job. He needs someone to fill in for him when he has things to do with Ashley or goes home to Eketahuna. He's got an interest in a property in Moewai, which isn't far from Eketahuna. Josh needs someone trustworthy to look after his interests in Auckland."

"I worry about you when you're overseas."

Cullen squeezed her. "I'm well-trained and work with a great team. We prepare as much as we can, given the circumstances. I think of you when we're apart and worry too."

"About me?" she asked in surprise.

"You've mentioned a couple of dates you've gone on in your emails. My imagination tells me any man with half a brain will see the treasure you are and snap you up before I get a chance. You didn't tell me about Dipstick. He came as an unpleasant surprise."

"The last six months have been busy. I haven't emailed any of my friends—not as often as I used to."

"I'm not blaming you," Cullen said. "I haven't been the best correspondent either."

Grace yawned, slapping her hand over her mouth a few seconds too late.

"You're tired. Let's try to sleep because we have a busy day tomorrow."

Grace nodded and got comfortable while Cullen turned off the bedside lamp, plunging them into intimate darkness.

"Your answer wasn't a *hell, no*, so I figure I won't upset you too much if I cuddle," he said after a while.

Grace recalled the previous night and winced.

"Sorry," Cullen said with a hard sigh. "I don't mean to pressure you."

Grace considered everything he'd said, the blunt truths he'd given her while making himself vulnerable. Jeff had never had a conversation like that with her. *Never.* "I'd like a cuddle," she said before she could second-guess herself.

"Thank fuck," Cullen muttered, and two seconds later, he had his arms wrapped around her while she lay with her back pressed against his chest. At first, she held her muscles tensely, but Cullen's even breathing suggested he'd fallen asleep. She allowed the tension to slide away and thought over everything he'd told her. He'd glossed over losing his friends, but she'd sensed the deep well of emotion inside him. Their deaths had shaken him and turned him more introspective.

She'd always liked Cullen, but their age difference and the fact she'd babysat him had made him out of bounds. She'd never contemplated the possibilities. He was a strong, good-looking man who turned heads when he walked down a street. Confidence radiated from him, yet he didn't pose or act with superiority. Best of all, he never treated women like objects. She'd met women he'd dated, although not recently. *Oh!* Most of those women had borne serious curves.

Points for Cullen. He would never put her down. Not like Jeff, who'd excelled at making her feel stupid and insecure. Small. Good enough to steal from, though.

Wow, she was such an idiot. When he'd started changing and putting her down more, she should've wised up faster.

While she'd told Cullen she had age and fertility concerns, the truth was her biological clock ticked louder each year. *Tick. Tick. Tick.* It had been part of why she'd rushed into the relationship with Jeff.

If only she'd listened to the tiny voice that had muttered this thing with Jeff was too fast. Oh, he'd been wily. He'd said and done everything to convince her they'd have a brilliant marriage—a blissful future. Heck, discovering him with Julia had hurt so badly, yet if she were honest with herself, it had been her pride, not her heart that had cracked.

A telling truth.

Grace allowed herself to consider Cullen again. Trustworthy—that was never a doubt. But what about when they grew older?

"Grace," Cullen grumbled. "I can hear your mind whirling and tumbling. Men live shorter lives than women. A fact. Now, can you please stop worrying and try to sleep?"

"I wasn't moving."

"Your brain is going a hundred miles an hour. If you don't stop, I'll take drastic measures."

Intrigue bombarded her. Feminine curiosity. "Like what?"

Cullen rolled without warning, and the next second, he'd levered over her and was smiling down into her face. Given the darkness, she couldn't see much more than an outline.

"This," Cullen said, and he kissed her.

While he'd kissed her before, not a single one of his kisses had rocked her like this one. He didn't hesitate or start gently. His lips mastered hers and demanded her response. At first, she tensed, but he wasn't rough, despite his confidence and clear experience. Her mind screeched to a halt. She did not want to imagine Cullen kissing other women.

That told her everything she wanted to know.

Grace stretched her arms and gripped his shoulders. He tensed until she made it obvious she was keeping him close rather than pushing him away. Ah, his confidence was a front.

Cullen licked the seam of her lips, urging her to part and allow him entry. Grace groaned, and her pulse spiked when Cullen's tongue did a sensual dance against hers. Decadent darts of pleasure swirled through her as Cullen gentled the kiss and took it to slow and dreamy.

When Cullen pulled back, they were both breathing hard.

"I've imagined kissing you like that loads of times." The backs of his fingers stroked over her cheek. "It was my favorite way to pass the time."

Grace licked her lips, a slow smoothing of her tongue across her tender mouth. "I think," she said, "that the actual kissing might be *my* favorite way to pass the day."

11

PONDERING OPTIONS

"Fuckin' bitch." Jeff glowered at his phone and started to put the call through again before reconsidering. She wouldn't answer. The stupid woman was growing a spine now when he needed her cooperation most.

What to do?

He strode the length of the dingy motel room while he considered the possibilities.

1. He was almost positive she had the gnome statue with her since he hadn't recovered it from Royce, the arsehole who'd helped himself to Jeff's gear.

2. Grace should be back in a week because that was all the time her boss had allowed her.

Why Grace continued to toil for the dictator, he had no clue. She worked crazy hours, which, although it had suited his purposes, wasn't any life at all. Also, the woman called Grace in to cover absences all the time, often at brief notice.

Where was Grace? Her parents hadn't arrived, so he assumed Grace had called them to say the wedding was off. Perhaps she'd gone to stay with them for a few days.

This neighbor guy who'd been with her when he'd watched the camera feed might be a problem. Jeff hadn't seen him before, but he'd asked Julia.

She'd told him the guy's name was Cullen Turner, and he was away a lot because he was in the army. Julia's mood had hovered at snippy, and it was apparent to Jeff she'd made a pass at the guy, and the dude had shot her down.

Army guy. *Not so great.* He'd notice things Grace hadn't. *Bugger.* The plan had been solid, and now it had gone to shit.

Jeff paced another circuit, wrinkling his nose at the stale remnants of cigarette smoke layered with a damp carpet fragrance.

Normally, he'd never stay in a dump like this—five-star hotels all the way for him. But, right now, because of Grace, his money supply had dried up, and he'd had to pay every available bit of cash to his boss to stay alive and healthy.

His boss didn't stand for non-payment. He'd been very clear about the consequences at the outset of his employment.

He muttered a curse under his breath and continued to ponder his options.

3. He could locate Grace and retrieve the gnome.

4. He could cut town using his false passport, which thank all the gods, he'd had with him.

Jeff slowed to a halt. This option would mean cutting his losses and starting over again. An attractive option, but if his boss caught him... He'd order him dead without a single regret. No one would ever find his body.

Not his preferred option. No, running was the last tick on his to-do list.

A grunt of recognition escaped.

Basically, he had to find Grace and retrieve his stash, which he could then sell to recoup his costs. He could pay his boss the rest of his profit, and everyone would be happy.

Except for Grace.

By the time he finished with her, she'd rue the day she'd stolen from him.

This entire situation was her fault. A man liked sex. He enjoyed variety, and especially when the sex between him and his lady was lackluster. A woman couldn't expect a man to go through life with frustration burning his gut.

"Grace should've been happy with the status quo," he muttered. "But no. She had to louse up this brilliant setup and create trouble. Bloody women. Typical! More trouble than they're worth."

12

PLAYING TOURIST

CULLEN HAD BEEN FIRM when he called a halt after a few kisses. Grace smiled as she pulled on shorts and a T-shirt, ready for their day of exploration. And it hadn't been because he hadn't wanted her. His erection had pressed against her backside in an entirely satisfactory way.

A bang on the door halted her daydreaming. "Hurry, Grace. You should know for future reference I'm a grumpy bear if I don't get my morning coffee."

She opened the door and beamed at him. "I could kiss and make it better."

He blinked, and she grinned at the brief flash of shock on his face before his expression smoothed to impassive.

"You've created a monster," she teased.

"I'm the grumpy beast because I lack caffeine in my system."

Grace took his hand and threaded her fingers with his.

She led him to the door. "What do you do while you're soldiering in the middle of nowhere? Do you have coffee there?"

"I have caffeine tablets in the case of an emergency. I prefer not to take them unless I'm desperate."

"Huh," Grace said and dragged him from their room. She waited while he locked the door and pocketed the key. To her immense satisfaction, Cullen reached for her hand without her needing to hint. Full of contentment, Grace ambled along the deck at Cullen's side. Both appreciated the sparkling sea panorama and the surrounding gardens. A bee hovered above a lavender bush, its industrious buzz competing with the morning chorus of a bird hiding in the massive trees behind the lodge.

"It's nice to take time to smell the flowers and appreciate nature," Grace murmured seconds before they entered the breakfast room. Several other couples were already at the table and chatting over their continental breakfasts.

"I never have time," Cullen said.

"Me neither. Sit," Grace said. "I'll get you a mug of coffee."

"You don't have to wait on me."

"I know," she whispered. "Why don't you grab us a juice each? I'll take either apple or orange, but nothing with mango, thanks. I drank lots of mango juice when I was sick one time, and I haven't been able to drink it since."

Cullen lifted his fingers to caress her cheek. "I adore learning these small things about you."

Grace grinned. "Me too. I'd better grab that coffee." At the tea and coffee station, she poured a large mug of coffee for Cullen and a smaller cup of tea for herself. It was lovely not having to rush around and cook for other people. Her boss took advantage of her good nature—Grace admitted that—but hadn't worried too much because she enjoyed work. Lately, though—the last two or three months when she'd wanted to do wedding stuff and reduce her hours, her boss had turned snappy at her requests.

It was time to take stock, Cullen's words from the previous night giving her a boost of confidence. The fledgling idea she'd shelved because of fear she wasn't capable kept poking its head out of the corner where she'd shoved it. It was a great idea, a winner, and she resolved to discuss it with Cullen this coming week to see what he thought. He'd give her his honest opinion.

"Here you go," she said.

Cullen clasped her hand and kissed the back of it.

"Do you want cereal and fruit?"

"I'll get mine in a minute. Let me savor my first cup of coffee, woman." His eyes crinkled at the corners as he said this.

"Aw," the older woman sitting opposite them said. "Newlyweds. You look so happy."

Startled, Grace opened her mouth to refute the assumption but stopped when Cullen squeezed her fingers in a warning. Neither of them wore rings. It was easier to let everyone assume they were a couple and forgo nosy questions from strangers.

So instead of replying, she merely smiled and wandered off to get cereal and fruit.

"What's first on our list today?" Cullen asked when she

settled on the chair beside him with her muesli. "I couldn't remember what you said." He lowered his voice. "I haven't been sleeping well. It always takes me weeks to settle into normal sleep patterns. The last couple of nights with you sharing the bed seem to have helped."

"I'm glad," she murmured. "We're doing a bus tour at ten and going fishing for blue cod this afternoon." She rubbed her hands together. "Blue cod is my absolute favorite fish to eat. Have you had it before? It's a cold-water fish and very expensive up in Auckland. Around the same price as snapper."

"Works for me," Cullen said. "I haven't fished for years. I used to go with my brothers."

"Is Devon still in Australia?"

"Yeah." Cullen sighed. "Things changed after Isaac died in the accident. Our family fell apart. I was lucky to have Gran."

"I miss her," Grace said. "She left me her special book full of family recipes."

"She couldn't have left them to a better person," Cullen said. "Thanks for reminding me. I can order some of my favorites when we get home."

"You'll need to be on your best behavior."

Cullen winked at her, his genuine grin darkening his blue eyes. "Always with you."

Grace swallowed, her pulse racing, not because of what he said, but more because of what he implied with his beautiful gaze and his sexy wink.

After breakfast, they grabbed what they would need for the day and stashed it in Cullen's day pack before setting off down the hill.

"My butt muscles are sore," Grace said. "Is it polite to mention that?"

"From walking up and down the hill?"

"I think so."

"I'll give you a massage later. That and another hot bath should do the trick."

Grace sent Cullen an appalled glance. "You're not looking at my butt. It's my least attractive part."

"Says who?"

"Me."

He clapped a hand over her mouth. "Now that's just a dare. I'll have to kiss your butt now."

No! That would never do. "The bus leaves from near the jetty. It's close to where we have to go to catch the fishing boat."

"Nice save," Cullen said with a chuckle, his fingers brushing across the cupcake tattoo on her left inner wrist.

The bus trip didn't take long since there were only thirty-two kilometers of road on the island. It did, however, orientate them.

"That's the rugby field where the kiwis sometimes come out at night," Grace said. "It's not far from our lodge."

"We're going to make a stop here," the young blond man who drove their bus said over the speaker system. "If you follow that path over on our left, you'll arrive at Observation Rock. From there, you'll get fantastic views, and it's also the best seat in town for watching the sunset."

She and Cullen followed the rest of the passengers and found a space to stand and study the view. A pair of olive-brown kaka, one of New Zealand's noisy parrot species, flew overhead with a flash of their red underwings. They disappeared into the treetops, their loud, demanding squawks ringing out.

"This is beautiful," Grace murmured. She savored Cullen's arm around her shoulders as she took in Ulva Island in the distance, a few boats dotting the sea and the glorious native bush around them. Seabirds wheeled overhead while behind her, a diminutive fantail flitted around, catching bugs on the wing. A plump wood pigeon cooed in a tree to her right.

They filed back to the bus, and Cullen took her hand, keeping her close and enjoying the physical contact as much as her. She kept thinking this was a dream—a spectacular one—because she still couldn't believe Cullen wanted her. He wasn't a man to lie, so she had to respect his words.

He wanted her.

She was going to get hurt. She knew it, but maybe this once, she'd jump in with both feet and ask questions later. With Jeff, she'd done everything right, yet nothing satisfying had come of their relationship.

"Hey." Cullen tapped the side of her head with his forefinger. "Don't deliberate too hard and get serious on me. That never bodes well."

She gave him honesty, something that had been lacking in her last relationship. She wanted to start this time—heck, she was going to do this. "I'm scared," she muttered, unable to meet his gaze. "What if I mess up and lose your friendship? It's important to me."

"Hey. What if getting together is the best thing for both of us? Think positive, okay?"

"I'll try."

"That's all I ask for. How about we walk up to the rugby field and do one of the short walks the bus driver mentioned around there? We can work out where to do our kiwi spotting during one of our free nights."

"Sounds good. The fishing tour leaves at two, or at least that's the meeting time at the boat."

Grace grunted and silently groaned her way up the slight incline leading to the start of the walk. "Cullen, when we get home, please nag at me to do more exercise. Work and standing on my feet all day in a busy kitchen isn't doing much to aid my stamina."

"You don't enjoy exercise like I do," he said with a grin. "You've told me many a time."

"I know." She sighed. "But I'm determined to walk more."

Cullen slowed his strides and grasped her hand. Grace's pulse rate blipped, but contentment also settled over her. The tension that had resided on her shoulders since discovering Jeff and Julia together eased away. "Instead of forcing yourself to go to the gym or run or attend an aerobics class..." He grinned at her. "You haven't discovered a love of aerobics yet, have you?"

"No. Definitely not. The last time I attended the class was full of beanpoles who wore designer lycra. I stood out, and their stares stabbed my back the entire time."

"Designer lycra, huh?"

Grace shuddered. "Some of their outfits looked as if they

wouldn't go over my arm, let alone a leg or a torso."

Cullen shook his head as he led her on to the start of the path. "I was going to suggest you do an activity where there is exercise. You still like to dance, right?"

"Yes, but what do you mean?"

"Remember, I suggested signing up for an activity? Maybe a line dancing class or you could try bowls or water aerobics. Even darts or eight-ball. You don't have to get fit, but the activity means you're socializing instead of staying at home feeling miserable. Try a few things not related to your work. Maybe join a group to do that walking in your future. You might find walking with others helps with your motivation."

Grace nodded and followed Cullen along the path and into the native bush. Immediately, the scent of rotten leaves and logs reached her along with a crisp green fragrance that put a pep in her step. "That makes sense. Wow, it's so beautiful in here."

Trees and ferns battled for space, some tall and spindly trees more trunk than leaves as they sought the sunlight. Beneath the canopy, moss grew on some trees while vines twisted around others.

It was cooler under the trees, Grace's skin pebbling with the drop in temperature. She zipped up her lightweight jacket and snapped photos with her phone.

Cullen also took photos, some with her posing in front of trees or ferns and one at a waterfall.

"Line dancing is a great idea. When we return to Auckland, I'll check out the local classes. Hopefully, I can find one to fit into my work schedule."

Five minutes later, they reached the sports area. Bush surrounded the rugby field on three sides and the road on the fourth side.

"It's close to the lodge," Grace said. "I thought it was farther, although this hill might challenge me."

"I'll hold your hand," Cullen promised.

By common consent, they returned to the village via the road and stopped at the Kai Kart, the local fast-food joint, for a meal of fish and chips for lunch. Grace sat at a picnic table and savored every flaky mouthful of blue cod and each crisp chip. She licked her fingers, enjoying the bite of salt contrasting with the delicate white flesh of the fish. Of course, the crunchy batter was perfect too.

A groan from Cullen, who was sitting opposite, had her glancing up in surprise. "Is something wrong?"

"Woman, stop with the breathy, sexy sighs, and for the love of all that is mighty, please stop licking your fingers."

She stilled with a digit halfway to her mouth. "What? Why?"

He leaned across the wooden table and took her lips in a demanding and passionate kiss. Sensations roared through her, communicating to each erogenous zone before ricocheting back and causing a stormy upheaval of confusion in her mind. Too soon, the kiss was over, but Cullen hadn't straightened yet. He sat with a mere whisper of distance between their lips.

Grace was uncomfortably aware of the group of workmen who'd sat at the nearest picnic table to them. The men kept winging curious glances their way, and Grace couldn't work out why. Heat rushed into her cheeks.

"The reason you need to stop is that watching you licking your fingers is torture. I'm as hard as a stone, and you're not helping me settle down any."

"Oh." She tried to wrap her mind around his words and failed.

Cullen released a strained chuckle. "Cupcake, you still don't get it, do you? You have power over me."

"B-but..." She trailed off, words failing her, and sought for a way to ease her discomfort. None of her former boyfriends had spoken with this bluntness, nor had she stirred them sexually. It was difficult to fathom. "Um..."

Cullen placed his hand over hers and squeezed briefly before leaning back to continue his meal. "These are great fish and chips. Some of the best I've ever had."

"Exactly," Grace exclaimed, a touch defensive now. She hadn't meant to discombobulate him. "Isn't discombobulate a brilliant word?"

Cullen laughed, his blue eyes dancing as he grinned at her. "It perfectly describes what you do to me."

Grace wrinkled her forehead. "But you're so confident. A soldier."

His humor faded, leaving an intensity behind that made her uneasy. "Soldiers have emotions too."

"I didn't mean to imply otherwise."

"You have the power to hurt me too, cupcake."

Her mouth rounded in an O of surprise as she stared at him. "I hadn't considered that," she said slowly. "And I should have, which makes me a selfish cow. My concern was for my needs and feelings. I forgot about you." She frowned. "Is that my problem? Not putting myself out there?"

"Possibly, but from my point of view, it kept you from connecting too deeply with another man before you were ready to give me serious consideration." He flashed a smile. "Now, if that makes me a selfish pig, I don't care."

"I'll try to do better and think of you too," she promised.

"I'd like that, cupcake. Are you finished?"

"Yes, do you want to wander around the museum until it's time to catch the fishing boat?"

"Sounds like a plan." Cullen wadded their fish and chip paper into a ball and stood to take it to the trash.

Grace paused a moment to watch him move, something she'd never allowed herself before. The confidence he radiated snared the attention of others. His fit and robust physique drew a second glance because Cullen was a man in his prime. She sighed, hardly able to believe he wanted her.

"Wow. Pinch me if I'm dreaming," she muttered. Just thinking about shedding her clothes and letting Cullen touch her brought a rush of warmth and arousal. It shot through her body, frisking tender places on the way. Briefly, her courage faltered, but she remembered she'd made a promise to Cullen. No more doubting. She was a capable woman who, for some reason, was beautiful in Cullen's eyes.

Bring on tonight.

13

KISSING AND OTHER STUFF

"THAT WAS FUN," GRACE said. "I haven't been fishing for ages, not since I was a teenager, and Dad and my uncle would take us out on the boat."

"You haven't lost the knack," Cullen said, nudging her shoulder with his as they wandered past the pub and toward the looming hill. He carried a bag of fish and another of supplies since they'd decided to cook at the lodge.

Grace raised her right hand and sniffed. "I smell like a fish."

"A little," Cullen agreed. "But I do too. We'll have a shower."

"We'll look like fish soon with all the blue cod we've been eating."

A seagull soared overhead and dive-bombed another bird that had found a tidbit on the beach. Gradually the incline increased, and Grace issued a gusty sigh.

"I'm exhausted. The only thing that's keeping me moving is the thought of the shower and a large glass of wine at the top of the hill."

"We're almost halfway already."

"Yeah. I wonder what the people living in that house are having for dinner. Whatever it is, their meal smells amazing. My guess is something with a tomato base. I detect the green herbs and fresh tomatoes."

"Perhaps they're making tomato sauce to have with their potato chips."

Grace snorted. "If you said that in the café, half of our customers would stare at you in confusion. That would be ketchup and French fries."

Cullen grinned. "People who live elsewhere in the world should embrace differences instead of expecting the rest of the world to fall in with their vernacular."

"*Yup*, that works in a busy café."

"Almost at the hilltop."

"My aching butt muscles know!" Grace climbed the three steps leading to the deck and issued a relieved sigh. "Ugh! I can't wait to get rid of this fishy smell."

"Do you want to toss for who goes first?" His brows arched as he waited for her reply.

"I thought you'd be a gentleman and let me go first."

His eyes gleamed, capturing her attention, and she wished she could read his mind. "We could share."

Grace plucked the keys from the side pocket of the daypack, her hair thankfully screening her expression while she unlocked the door. Share a shower?

She'd never done that before and wasn't sure she wanted Cullen to...

No! He'd expect her to backtrack. It was his way of getting the first shower. She twisted the key and opened the door. "Okay."

She didn't see his expression. Truthfully, she was frightened to look, but she heard his soft chuckle and got the sense she'd surprised him. *Excellent.* He kept her off-balance, and it wouldn't hurt him to suffer the same fate.

"I'll put the fish in the fridge," Cullen said. "Do you want that wine before or after the shower?"

"After. I can't wait to wash my hair." Grace grabbed a set of clean underwear, a plain pink T-shirt, and a pair of black leggings. With determined steps, she strode to the bathroom. She stripped off her dirty, fishy shorts and T-shirt and left them in a pile in the corner.

After this morning, she knew the water took a while to heat, but she didn't care. She stepped around the glass that partitioned the wet area of the bathroom, turned on the water, and let it run over her body. The chill had her wincing, but she sucked it up and grabbed the bar of soap.

A jolt ran through her when a pair of masculine hands claimed the soap from her. Although Cullen had mentioned sharing, she hadn't been one-hundred percent clear of his next move.

He ran the soap over her shoulders and down her spine, a tingling sensation chasing the direction of his hands and fingers. Grace closed her eyes.

It seemed they were doing this.

She opened her mouth to object, hesitated, and pressed her lips together to contain her protest. Cullen would do nothing against her will—a given because he was and had always been an honorable man.

She sighed, still with her eyes firmly closed. Her lack of sight amplified her other senses, and a low-level electrical charge danced across her skin. Impossible, of course, but that was what Ms. Touch screamed at her. Ms. Hear gloried in Cullen's low chuckle, a shiver pushing through her.

"Cullen," she whispered, propelled by Ms. Speech to react while Ms. Sight pleaded with Grace to open her eyes to inspect some of that soldier manliness. Was his butt high and tight and capable of forward propulsion? Were his thighs strong enough to carry her from danger? Did he have a pretty c—? Grace gasped and speedily redirected her thoughts. That was what happened when she read books about male/female attraction. She absorbed many weird facts.

"You have an A-class arse, Gracie." Cullen was so close his warm breath feathered her ear. And she gained superior knowledge of his cock since it prodded her. She might not know if it was pretty, but it functioned perfectly and seemed impressively large. "Turn around. Let me see all of you."

Grace gulped but followed Cullen's suggestion.

Look at his dick, Ms. Sight implored. Grace swallowed hard and stared into Cullen's blue eyes, searching for...

Heck, she had nothing.

This situation was way beyond anything she'd imagined.

"Gracie, don't go shy on me now," Cullen whispered. "Step away from me a fraction so I can look at you."

Grace sucked in a breath for courage and stepped back into the stream of water. For an instant, her hair blinded her, and Cullen's amusement at her plight echoed around them.

"You intended to wash your hair, right?"

"Yes," she said, attempting to clear her vision. With her gaze downward, the first thing she spotted was Cullen's cock. *Ooh! It is pretty*, Ms. Sight declared. Grace bit back a groan, instantly imagining Cullen filling her. Her sex throbbed.

"Grace, look at me," Cullen ordered, but his voice was gentle and non-threatening. "You're gorgeous, and I can't wait to touch every inch of you, to taste the flesh between your legs and watch you come apart for me."

"I..." Before she could speak, Cullen placed his fingers over her lips.

"I'm looking forward to you touching me in return. Tasting me."

Their gazes met, and she noticed Cullen's eyes had darkened. It made her realize he truly wanted her since a man couldn't fake desire.

He dipped his head and claimed her lips in a lazy kiss that pushed passion through her and amped up her longing. She shivered again, but this time, it was the heat that sizzled through her that caused the conflagration.

Cullen broke off the kiss way too soon, and she frowned at him, still craving more of his mouth.

"Let me wash your hair for you," he suggested. "Then

you can start drying it while I scrub myself clean. You have five minutes at most before I take you to bed and fuck you until you scream with pleasure."

Grace's mouth fell open as she stared up into his hot, dark gaze. "I thought we were having dinner."

"Later. Right now, I'd prefer to feast on your sexy body. I've waited for this for a long time, and my patience has worn thin. No, wait, I promised you time. If you need to wait longer, that's what we'll do, okay?"

Grace continued to stare at Cullen, a little bemused but turned on by his explicit words. She managed a nod.

"Shampoo?" he prompted.

She reached for the sample the lodge provided without another word.

Seconds later, Cullen had rubbed in the shampoo until it lathered. He was gentle, yet his touch was firm, and Grace's eyes slid closed while she enjoyed the scalp massage.

"Do you use conditioner?"

Grace's eyes flew open. Most men wouldn't know about hair conditioners. Jeff certainly wouldn't have—not that they'd ever showered together.

"Grace?"

"Yes, please." She plucked the conditioner bottle from the shelf and handed it to Cullen.

After rinsing her hair, he applied the conditioner and gave her another massage before washing away the residue. Pure bliss. It took her a while to jolt back to the program since she'd zoned out on pleasure.

Cullen's hand slid down her spine and came to rest on

a buttock. He gave her another one of those unhurried, sexy kisses that drove every thought from her head before setting her firmly away from him.

"If you don't want a wet pillow, you'd better dry your hair. This is your five-minute warning unless you want more time. Cupcake?"

"What?" She shook herself and blinked up at his sexy face.

"Five minutes or more time," he repeated.

"Okay, I'll dry my hair." She stepped from the shower and grabbed a towel to blot the worst of the water from her body. She'd barely started the blow-drier when Cullen appeared by her side. He wore not a stitch of clothing, and it was easy to discern his confidence.

He feared nothing.

Not judgment. Not her.

"Want that glass of wine now? Maybe some cheese and biscuits?"

"Sounds lovely," she said and smiled, although the sentiment didn't quite fit her lips. This entire situation with Cullen had her teetering off-balance.

Did she want to call a halt and wait?

No. That would be a *hell no.*

In the mirror, she watched Cullen prowl to the tiny kitchen area. "Wow," she whispered, and with an Alice-falling-down-the-rabbit-hole sensation riding her, she set about drying her hair.

Anticipation roared through her, making her hand shaky and the need to hurry real. She didn't make it to five minutes before turning off the drier and calling her damp hair done.

On quivering legs, she stood, pulled on one of the provided robes. Cullen had drawn the curtains, turning the bedroom into a secluded haven.

Grace swallowed hard. Was she truly going to do this? A beat and one shaky step later, she concluded she was, and judging by the gleam in Cullen's eyes, he was more than ready.

She didn't want to wait, she realized. Now that Cullen had made her see the possibilities... Heck, he'd blindsided her with his proposal, but he truly wanted her, and that was a heady thing.

"I like you better without clothes," Cullen said.

"It's weird wandering around naked." Jeff had never strutted around with Cullen's confidence, not that she intended to mention that aloud.

"True, but the view is great."

Her gaze ran over Cullen's handsome face before dipping lower to study his chest. "I thought you might have tattoos."

"I'm not anti-tattoos, but I've never found something I'd like on my skin permanently. Come here."

She wandered closer, and he grasped her hand and tugged her onto the bed.

"Your cupcake tattoo is meaningful, and you got it to commemorate your win in the baking contest. It's small and cute." His thumb stroked over the tattoo, which sat on her left inner forearm. Her breath caught, and a shiver ran up her arm. His touch was magical, doing things to her body.

"Come and sit here by me. Get yourself comfortable." His husky voice thrilled her and pushed another tremble of arousal through her body.

She gave an audible gulp, and he stilled.

"Are you frightened of me?"

"No," she retorted. "What I am is nervous. Part of me still wonders if this is such a brilliant idea."

He pressed his fingers to her lips, and in a flash of daring, she licked them. It was his turn to gasp. His blue eyes darkened to indigo.

"Maybe we'll have our wine and snacks later," he muttered. "Both of us will do better if we take off the edge." With that said, he moved with speed. He tugged the belt of her robe, and she was naked before she could blink.

Then Cullen was over her, pinning her to the mattress with clear intent etched into his features.

"You are driving me crazy, woman." His mouth caressed hers. "This is your final chance to tell me you don't want this."

Grace considered saying no for two seconds. *No!* She was sticking to her brave, determined self. "I want you."

"Thank god," Cullen muttered and settled in to kiss her properly. He teased and stroked, and each brush of his mouth and sweep of his tongue did things to her libido. Never had she experienced such need, and he'd barely started. *Oops.* He wouldn't want her at all if she continued to lay there like a log without reciprocation. It was time to assuage her curiosity. She ran her hand down his back and squeezed one taut buttock.

Cullen groaned.

Emboldened, she explored more of his spectacular muscles. His back. His biceps. His backside.

Cullen paused in kissing her to groan again. "Grace, I love your hands on me."

"Turn over," she suggested. "Let me explore your chest."

Cullen gave her one deep, passionate kiss that had her gasping and gripping his shoulders for purchase before he pulled back. He showcased his strength in the quick way he rearranged their bodies, lifting her, so she straddled his lean hips.

"Such a beautiful view," he whispered. "I love these." He cupped her breasts and squeezed them gently before rubbing her nipples between his fingers and thumbs.

Grace arched her back, offering more of herself. She wriggled, her backside brushing Cullen's erection. In response, Cullen pinched her nipple, and the tiny arc of pain rippled downward to land in the achy spot between her thighs.

"Cullen," she whispered.

"Grace, you're gorgeous. I've wanted you for years, and I can't believe you're here with me now." And with that said, he flipped her onto her back again.

"Hey," she protested. "I haven't had my turn."

"Later," he promised. "I'm hanging onto my sanity by a thread. I want to make this good for you, so you'll want to have sex with me for the rest of the week, the month." He paused. "Until I go back to work."

Before Grace could even process his words, he settled in to explore her body, seeming to delight in her curves. He kissed. He nipped. He soothed the sting with the press of his fingers or the flat of his tongue. In return, Grace kissed him back whenever he aimed his lips at her mouth. She ran her fingers over his back and shoulders and did some nipping of her own.

"I have to taste you. Your scent is driving me crazy."

"I've never driven anyone crazy before."

He snorted. "You underestimate yourself, cupcake." With that said, he parted her legs and gave her a long lick that had her lifting her hips into the sensation and groaning her enjoyment.

"Oh, Cullen," she whispered. Her eyes fluttered closed, and she shivered, the beginnings of an orgasm enthralling her. She never came this fast. *Never.* She gulped as Cullen teased her clit and cried out when the sensations gathered to a fiery point and exploded through her. Cullen continued to lick her, but more gently as she floated down from her climax.

"Wow," she whispered.

"More where that came from," Cullen said, sounding proud of himself.

Grace laughed, and that wasn't something she remembered ever doing after sex with Jeff. Half of the time, he hadn't even bothered to ensure she'd enjoyed their lovemaking.

And that was enough of Jeff. Cullen was right. She wouldn't waste any more of her thoughts on the horrid man.

"Grace?" Cullen scowled at her and tapped her backside with one big hand. "If you're thinking about Scumbag, stop! It's rude and not complimentary to me."

"No, it's all you, Cullen. Promise. When can we do that again?"

Cullen winked at her. "That spectacular, huh?"

"Cullen." Grace beamed at him, lighthearted and happier than she'd been for ages. She aimed a kiss at his mouth, but what started as teasing fun morphed into passion. Cullen groaned, and Grace clung, diving deep into pleasure. Cullen kissed her again and again until she was breathless and desperate for more. But despite Cullen's apparent urgency, he still took the time to explore her body, suck on her nipples and tease her to the point of madness.

"Cullen," she whispered, her voice hoarse with need.

Cullen leaned over to grab his wallet. "We have to make the most of this because I only have one condom right now." After ripping the foil packet with his teeth, he rolled the latex onto his shaft. "Ready?" he asked, his gaze intent.

"Yes," Grace said without hesitation.

Cullen braced on his arms and pushed into her. Grace groaned at the fullness and the intimacy of being the focus of Cullen's attention.

He took his time, withdrawing and thrusting back home. Each stroke pushed bliss through her, the exquisite sensations making her head whirl. This spectacular sex-god was Cullen. Cullen, a man she'd never considered as a partner and one who'd sat under her nose the entire time.

She reached up to kiss him, savoring the contact as she climbed toward another climax. Wow. *Just wow.*

Sometimes she never came once, let alone twice.

Cullen stopped his thrusts, buried deep inside her. He tapped her temple. "Mind on me," he snapped.

"It is," she promised. "Believe me, it is totally on you. Cullen, yes! Please keep doing that."

The scowl left Cullen's face, his smile breathtaking. He caressed her lips, his tongue moving in time with his strokes. His pace quickened, and he hit the perfect spot. Grace detonated, ecstasy exploding across her senses.

Cullen pumped into her for three quick strokes and stilled, his face taut, eyes closed, and his teeth bared as he climaxed. He stilled, and Grace's grip on his shoulders tightened.

Lovemaking had never been this wonderful experience in the past. She didn't know if it was because they were friends beforehand or if it was Cullen. Whatever the reason, Grace had never enjoyed lovemaking as much as this before. It was a bit of an eye-opener.

"What's wrong?" Cullen asked, his gaze enigmatic.

"I want to do that again," Grace said, her voice a little breathless as she grinned at him.

His return smile was a beautiful thing—a ray of brilliant sunshine wrapped in approval. "That can be arranged, but we'll have to buy condoms tomorrow."

Grace's stomach took that moment to release a deafening rumble of complaint. She and Cullen stared at each other and burst out laughing.

Cullen winked. "Perhaps we'll eat first."

Grace nodded, her lips quirking. "Sounds like the perfect plan."

14

CHASING GRACE

JEFF PACKED HIS GEAR and left the motel in the middle of the night before they realized he'd used a stolen credit card. That they hadn't run the card because their terminal was down had been a piece of luck. It was no hardship leaving the card with them. Damn flea-pit wasn't worth one-hundred dollars a night. He'd be glad to leave the stench of damp coming from the walls and the tobacco that had permeated the bedding, the peeling wallpaper, and the carpet.

From the motel, he grabbed a cab to the main street of the local town. After paying the driver cash, Jeff took a roundabout route and made frequent stops to study window displays. Finally, his meandering path took him toward the local travel interchange.

Rain tumbled from overhead, and the driving sleet cut through his flimsy jacket. The raindrops dripped off his concealing cap and ran down his neck. He cursed under his breath and hitched his pack higher on his shoulder.

This was Grace's fault, and he intended to take it out on her hide once he recovered the missing gnome. If he was wrong, and she didn't have it, he didn't know what to do next. Interrogate her, probably, because she was his only lead.

His damp clothes clung to his chest and shoulders. He ignored the discomfort, and after scanning the vicinity, pushed through the double doors and out of the elements. Hopefully, the men after him wouldn't think to search here because he'd been vocal about his hatred of public transport.

Needs must when the devil drives, as his English grandmother used to say. He had no other options.

With another muttered curse, this time about Grace's parentage, he approached the lone worker to discuss his travel options to Wellington. Finally, he purchased a bus ticket to the capital city since a coach was much cheaper than the train and settled into a hidden corner to while away the hours until his ride.

He must've fallen asleep because a grinding noise woke him: the shriek of brakes, the bang of the entrance doors, and the laughter of children. He jerked, his gaze darting to his wristwatch. Crap! He jumped to his feet and picked up his bag, charging outside to join the line of passengers waiting to board the bus.

His pulse raced at his near-miss. Hiding in Papakura for one day was doable, but two days was pushing his luck. His bosses wanted his head because he hadn't delivered on his promises. Oh, he intended to, but first, he had to grab Grace. In a fit of brilliance, he'd wondered if Grace had gone to Stewart Island on their honeymoon alone. A phone call to the lodge had confirmed this guess, although his phone call had gone unanswered when the manager had transferred it to the room. The manager hadn't given him the room number, but he'd figure that out once he arrived.

Chasing Grace was a long shot but his only option at this stage. His hidden camera had shown Grace picking up each of the statues. He'd seen her place three of them inside a box with his clothes and other gear, but the camera angle hadn't shown him the fate of the fourth gnome.

The ecstasy tabs in that statue were worth a fortune, a bloody massive profit to his bosses and a decent one for him. He must get his hands on the gnome. He could sell the pills anywhere—perhaps in Wellington. With the money in hand, the danger to him would reduce. It was hard to tell with Matthew, his immediate boss. The guy's unpredictability made him lethal, and Jeff held a healthy respect for him.

It was his turn to show his ticket, and he handed it over.

"Want to stow your bag?" the driver asked.

"No, I'll keep it with me," Jeff said.

"Get on." The driver jerked his head at the bus.

Jeff picked an aisle set toward the rear. Hopefully, he wouldn't need to share. His phone rang as he was stowing his bag in the overhead rack, and he gulped at the caller id displayed on his screen.

Matthew.

Hell, he should've turned off his phone. At least he'd had the sense to turn off the GPS. No one could track him that way. No, the trouble he was in now was deep enough. Ignoring his boss wouldn't make things much worse. He rejected the call, and this time, powered down the phone.

Jeff dropped onto his chosen seat and pulled his hat low while pretending to sleep. In truth, he came nowhere near rest with tension pushing his heartbeat to racy speeds. This was the most dangerous part of his plan. Once he'd left Auckland, he wouldn't need to remain as vigilant.

Anyone who knew him would suspect he'd head to the airport and book a flight. Now that he'd ignored his boss, Matthew would assume the worst, so Jeff *could not* fail in his quest to regain the drugs.

Once again, his mind slipped to Grace. He'd had a sweet thing going there, and she'd been worth the price of marriage. Men had never paid her attention, and she'd fallen into his trap like a ripe piece of fruit. A litany of his favorite curses flowed through his mind, his hands forming fists in his lap. This entire bullshit situation was Grace's fault. If she'd kept to her normal behavior, she wouldn't have walked into the bedroom and caught him with Julia.

Her rejection had pissed him off, and she'd pay for the slight. She'd pay for taking the statue or dumping it into the street. Either way, he'd exact his pound of flesh.

Grace had screwed up his grand scheme, and that would not do.

He ran through his flexible plan. He had enough cash for a flight from Wellington to Invercargill, or if this didn't work out, he'd make the rest of the journey by a combo of train and bus. Unfortunately, it wasn't safe for him to use his air miles since Matthew would have his contacts checking for that. Jeff could, however, use one of his false passports and pay cash. *Fuck that bitch.*

Jeff hated traveling with stinky passengers who weren't fit to wipe his designer shoes. That the situation forced him to lie low and travel this way...

Grace's fault.

Grace's fuckin' fault.

He eagerly anticipated getting his hands on her and making her sorry for mucking up the fantastic life he'd mapped out for himself when he was a teenager. She would fuckin' rue the day they'd met.

15

A GUESS PLAYS OUT

"Look," Grace whispered. "A black robin." She lifted her camera to snap a picture. They'd taken a tiny ferry to Ulva Island, and now she and Cullen wandered the quiet forest paths, searching for rare native birds that inhabited the pest-free island. "Bother." She lowered her camera as the bird flitted away to land on a high branch of a totara tree. "Did you get the shot?"

"Nope," Cullen said. "They're too quick."

"I'd say shy," Grace replied as they ambled onward, often stopping to study the rimu trees and other natives such as karaka and puriri with their broad branches and leaf cover blocking the sunshine. Ferns brushed their legs while the fallen leaves on the path crunched beneath their boots. Birds sang, and each time they spotted one, they halted for photos and sometimes consulted their bird book to identify the species.

"Cullen, thank you so much for suggesting you come to Stewart Island with me. I'm enjoying this trip so much more than I would've with—"

He slapped a hand over her mouth, his eyes gleaming with mischief. "Don't say the J-word."

"I have no intention of uttering that name," she said the instant Cullen removed his fingers. "What I meant is that you enjoy nature and walking as much as I do. You like taking photos."

"We have things in common," Cullen said, stepping close and brushing a lock of hair away from her eyes. "But I already knew this, which was why I pushed to come with you on this holiday."

She stood on tiptoe and pressed her lips to his, happiness flooding her because she could touch him whenever she wanted. He encouraged her and took the same enjoyment from the physical contact she did.

She smiled up at him. "We should keep walking or risk missing the return ferry." The smile that curled her lips next sure felt sly. "I'm a little tired, and it might be best if I had a nap to ensure I'm fighting fit and ready for kiwi spotting tonight."

"That smile of yours is ingenious," Cullen said, confirming her thoughts about her expression. "What did you have in mind?"

"A nap," she said, aiming for innocence.

A glance at his knowing grin suggested she'd failed at that too. "Am I invited to have a sleep with you?"

"Yes, I'd enjoy your company. I've decided it's more fun sharing a bed than sleeping alone. If the person I'm with is you, of course. I don't share with just any man."

"Excellent answer," Cullen said. "Over to your right in the tree. A saddleback."

He snapped his photo as Grace whirled, her camera lifted, ready to take the shot. Too late. The bird had already taken to the wing.

"Most of my photos are blurs. I hope I do better with the kiwi."

"We can share our photos. This isn't a competition." He checked his watch. "We should hustle. The wind has come up. It's going to rain."

"Do you think the kiwi trip will go ahead? They take us out on a boat to another part of the island."

"I'm not sure I'd enjoy the crossing between Bluff and Oban, but it shouldn't be too bad here. If the operators decide to cancel the trip, we'll walk up to the rugby field tonight."

"Brilliant Plan B," Grace said.

When they reached the ferry, the vessel bobbed energetically at its mooring. The thin stretch of water between Ulva and Stewart Island tossed and churned with noticeably larger whitecaps.

Grace felt the weight of a stare when Cullen took her hand and spotted two twenty-something women observing them. Heat sped to her cheeks, but one woman grinned and made fanning motions in front of her face. Her friend gave Grace a thumbs-up signal. The tension seeped from Grace's shoulders, and a feel-good grin formed on her lips. They weren't staring at her and Cullen because of their age difference or accusing Grace of cradle-snatching. That was her imagination.

Instead, they approved of Cullen, and Grace got the sense they envied her.

Cullen bent to whisper in her ear. "See. There is nothing wrong with us as a couple. The age difference between us is negligible."

"All aboard," the ferry pilot called.

The distance between Ulva and Stewart Island wasn't great, and ten minutes later, she and Cullen clambered off the silver ferry and set off for the short walk back to the lodge.

"Do you want to have lunch at the pub?" Cullen asked. "I'm starving this morning, even after breakfast."

"That would be because we never got around to eating a proper dinner," Grace said with a blush as she recalled exactly how they'd spent their evening.

"I wouldn't change it for anything." Cullen slipped his arm around her waist. "But I am hungry. I require nourishment to keep up my stamina, and we need to pick up some condoms."

"I admire your stamina," Grace said, keeping a straight face.

"More where that comes from," Cullen replied, his voice gruff. He opened his mouth in an exaggerated yawn. "I might require a snooze too, but only if you're there to help me sleep comfortably."

A peal of laughter escaped Grace even as she rolled her eyes.

At the back of her mind, a thought occurred. A truth. She'd never had this much fun with a male friend. The flirting. The touching. The kisses. Happiness pressed against her chest, and her smile grew so wide her mouth hurt.

Cullen merely patted her backside, letting his hand linger on her curves. "Please walk faster before I expire of hunger."

Obligingly, Grace lengthened her steps and didn't even complain about the slight elevation rise and her resulting breathlessness. Instead, she savored Cullen's closeness and wondered how she'd let him go when his vacation ended.

Jeff's legs trembled as the ferry pulled up to the jetty. Never a great sailor, the enormous waves had sent his stomach into revolt. He'd thrown up three times into a paper bag. People had stared at him, their disgust plain as they'd backed away. Jeff hadn't cared because his misery had consumed him. Even now that the rocking of the boat had ceased, he wavered unsteadily. He caught a whiff of vomit and grimaced at his hoodie. He'd missed the bag during one violent rock of the boat. His temper, which had been uncertain since he'd discovered his possessions sitting on the footpath, spiraled rapidly upward.

If only Grace had continued with her usual meek behavior, everything would've been all right. Instead, she suddenly got a mad hair and kicked him out when he'd needed his plan to run like a Swiss timepiece.

He trailed the passengers off the boat and wove through the massed crowd who waited for the crew to offload their luggage. With his day pack over his shoulder, he pulled his cap lower and wandered toward the backpacker's hostel. It was the cheapest accommodation available, given his budget, and he couldn't wait to ditch these clothes and shower.

Once he was clean again and had a drink, he'd feel more human.

Only then would he set about finding his traitorous fiancée and retrieving his property.

Jeff strolled along the footpath that curved around the bay. Waves—small ones, thankfully—rolled onto the white sand, and several groups of children were taking advantage of the low tide. Some searched for crabs or some other sea creature, while the second group of children built a castle fortress. Their joyous laughter floated in the air, but Jeff sniffed in disdain.

A flock of seagulls fought for pieces of bread, their noisy squawks cutting arrows of pain through Jeff's head. He hoped he'd find someone willing to donate a painkiller or two, otherwise he'd never shift this headache.

He noted a supermarket, a clothing shop, and a tourist booking place on the other side of the tarmac road.

Another street dissected the main one. A glance showed a café, a museum, and a wildlife conservation center. He crossed the road and slowed in front of the pub, a craving for alcohol filling him.

No. Looking and smelling the way he did would arouse curiosity. People would remember him. It was better to go with his original plan and clean up first.

He glanced through the window of the pub restaurant

and came to a standstill.

His bloody fiancée sat there eating a meal with a man. He glared at the man. Wait, was this the neighbor? He wasn't certain since this guy had shorter hair and while he had a beard, it was much lighter and groomed. More like scruff than the beard the neighbor had sported. As he watched, Grace plucked something off her plate and offered it to the man. The stranger kissed Grace's knuckles after he'd swallowed the food.

The bitch.

She had the bloody cheek to castigate him for sleeping with Julia, and she was down here cavorting with a man while enjoying their honeymoon without him.

The bitch.

The pounding in his ears exacerbated his headache, and when he glared at them, it was like staring down a tunnel. His muscles tensed, and he shook anew as he forced himself to move away from the window instead of confronting the cheating, lying bitch.

At least he knew she was here. If he hustled over his shower, he could return and follow her back to where she was staying. Once he discovered this, he'd plan to retrieve his statue.

While he wasn't confident she had it, his gut told him she'd taken it from the house. The silly woman probably didn't even realize the statue's value, and if he were lucky, he'd recover it and leave without her being any the wiser. Although he itched to strike and take revenge on the bitch, this was the more sensible course of action.

In and out.

Yeah, in and out, no matter how much he wanted to punch her in the face for causing this trouble and wrecking his smooth, ordered life.

Damn. His hands curled to fists. He'd been well on his way to taking over and running his territory instead of reporting to Matthew. Instead of taking cents when he could earn dollars.

Jeff spotted the signpost for the backpacker's place and checked in while trying to contain his disdain for the rundown accommodation. He was used to the best—the top hotels with twenty-four-hour service, minibars, and luxury. Sharing a room. Bah!

At least the shower was hot. After letting the water pour over his head for five minutes, his temper improved along with his confidence. He'd wanted to enjoy the shower for longer, but he needed to learn Grace's location. Not that this dump was large, but it'd make this process easier if he didn't have to search the entire Oban township.

Jeff pulled a clean hoodie out of his daypack and paired it with jeans and a T-shirt. He slapped his cap on his head and draped his daypack over his shoulder before he left his dorm.

Two women in their early twenties smiled at him in reception. He dipped his head in acknowledgment but kept walking. Time enough for women after this, once he had his statue back.

The breeze nipped at his cheeks, and a car rumbled past as he returned to the pub. He slowed as he approached and glanced through the window. They were gone.

Hell.

Did he go inside and risk meeting them face to face?

Jeff hesitated, lingering until he noticed a couple sitting inside the restaurant staring at him. *Crap.* He forced his legs to carry him past the pub and around the corner.

There they were.

The dude had his arm around Grace's podgy waist, and he was smiling at her as if she'd hung the stars in the sky. What the fuck? Grace wasn't much to look at with her red hair and stocky build. He preferred blondes who looked after themselves and visited the gym.

Come on. Where are you staying?

Jeff edged closer but got ready to cross the road if one of them turned or noticed him.

"The museum," he heard Grace say and groaned inwardly. *Great. Just great.* No way did he want to loiter. Damn, he wished he'd paid more attention to the plans she'd made for their honeymoon. She'd raved about the deal she'd got and what she'd wanted to do, but he'd ignored her rambling.

All he'd heard was Stewart Island, and he'd blanked because this was not his kind of holiday. Since he'd been in a delicate part of getting his hands on Grace's money, he hadn't wanted to cause an argument, and he'd let it go. He'd figured he could wriggle out of the honeymoon or at least seduce Grace into going somewhere more suitable.

More fool him.

He scowled as the couple entered the museum. Now that he'd had a better look at the dude, he recognized him. It was Grace's neighbor. The one that spent little time at home because of his job. Something to do with the military, Julia had told him. He'd changed the subject because he hadn't enjoyed the wistful note in Julia's voice.

She'd wanted this man, and now the bastard had his hands all over Grace.

Jeff wandered past the museum and considered that drink. No, he needed to follow Grace. If they had a place out of town and needed to drive, he'd have a tough time finding the couple again. After glancing around him, Jeff went to the café across the road from the museum. At least he could have a coffee and something to eat while he waited.

One hour later. One bloody excruciatingly long hour later, he spotted Grace and the man exit the museum. His gaze zapped to their clasped hands, and he wanted to curse, but he'd already attracted enough attention by sitting here for so long.

Jeff stood and left the cafe, sauntering and keeping well back.

The man was tall and fit in appearance. He radiated confidence, and Jeff would bet he knew what was happening around him, even though his attention centered on Grace.

He must want Grace's money. *Too late, buddy. I've already cleaned her out.*

The pair walked past the pub and took the road that led up a steep hill. Jeff groaned. They were the only people in sight, and if they glimpsed him, Grace might recognize him. A sneeze erupted from him, muffled at the last second by a hand slapped over his mouth.

He ducked behind a tree and sneezed again. This is why

he stuck to cities. The great outdoors brought out his allergies.

By the time he got himself under control, Grace and the man had disappeared.

"Fuck." This woman was pissing him off. He increased his pace and strode around the corner, his breath coming in harsh pants. Despite his sneezing and his lack of puff, he forced himself to keep moving. He caught a flash of movement up ahead and darted behind a bush. He waited three long seconds before he risked peeking from his cover.

To his right, a property clung to the crest of the hill. The building was long with a deck. Someone had taken care of the garden, and flowers crowded every available space. He remembered them from his granny's garden but had no inkling of the names. Some might call them pretty, and he supposed they were, but right now, all he wanted was to get his hands on that statue.

He scanned the area and saw not a single person. He crept forward, caution urging him to go slowly despite his need for haste. His boss would catch up with him eventually, and when he did, Jeff wanted to have the statue in hand to go with his explanation. Even then, he wasn't certain Matthew wouldn't have him killed. He swallowed hard at the thought.

That statue belonged to him, and even if Grace didn't have it with her, she might know where it was. He wouldn't allow her to fob him off again.

Somewhere above him, a door opened. He froze, trying to decide what to do. His shoulders slumped as he stopped himself from following his instinct to storm up there and slap Grace.

No, softly, softly.

He'd come back later tonight since he had a general idea of where they were staying. He'd skulk under cover of darkness and hopefully get his hands on that gnome.

16

WALKING WITH KIWIS

THE WIND DROPPED A fraction, but it was still blustery enough to make the boat trip to the kiwi location rocky. Grace sat beside Cullen, too excited to feel discomfort. Cullen dropped his arm along the back of her seat while they listened to their guides talk about what to expect once they reached the shore.

"First," Anna, their female guide, said, her attitude as perky as her pigtails. "Remember, these are wild birds. While we will do our best to find a kiwi for you to watch, nature doesn't perform on cue. I need you to walk behind me in a single file. Make sure you aim your flashlight at the ground, and the second I give the signal, please switch off your torch. Remain silent and walk as quietly as possible so we can hear the kiwi. The kiwi probes the ground with their beak to grab grubs, and the bird makes a snorting sound to clear their nostrils while they're feeding. We'll also check for the very distinctive kiwi tracks." She paused and smiled at her fellow guide, a tall and slender male with dreads.

"I will walk at the front while Steven brings up the rear. We don't want to lose any of you in the bush."

"Anna, where will we walk?" a rotund woman called from the rear.

Anna smiled and pointed at a map on the wall. "We're here." She pointed with her finger. "Once we've disembarked, we'll walk across here to the sea on the other side. The kiwis sometimes forage for worms on the beach. Now when we encounter a kiwi, I want to remind you to switch off your torches. I will highlight the bird with my special red light. The red light doesn't bother the kiwi, and he or she will continue to feed. No flash photography. You'll startle the bird, and it will retreat before everyone has time to see it." She smiled again. "Did everyone hear that? Repeat after me. No flash photography."

"No flash photography," two women at the front of the group chanted, making everyone laugh.

A few questions followed, and then the crew tied up the boat, and it was time to disembark.

Cullen held her right hand, the warmth of his palm against hers bringing a sense of peace to Grace. Cullen liked to touch her, and he did it often. Grace found she enjoyed his physicality and his lovemaking... Wow.

The truth was she was a little sore, but she wouldn't change this experience for anything.

"Got your camera ready?" Cullen asked.

"I need to turn off my automatic flash," Grace said,

trying to juggle her torch and her camera.

"Let me hold the flashlight," Cullen said.

"Bossy much?" she murmured as she handed it over to him.

Cullen snorted but aimed the light where she needed it. "Done," she said. "Let's hurry. They're moving out."

"Don't panic, cupcake. The group won't leave without us."

They were the last to join the line as everyone followed Anna in single file. Steven walked behind them.

"It doesn't matter where you are in the line," Steven murmured from behind them. "The kiwis are just as likely to appear next to us."

"Torches off," came the quiet command.

Everyone turned off their torches, and the excitement ramped up noticeably. No one spoke. Grace took in the scent of green leaves and the musty dampness of the forest floor. The wind rattled the leaves in the treetops while Grace scanned the area where Anna shone her torch. It bathed the trees and ground in an alien red light.

"Do you see anything?" she whispered to Cullen.

"There is something just to our right," Cullen said in a low voice to Steven.

Steven switched on his red light, and she saw the kiwi. Awe filled her, and Grace leaned against Cullen, content to watch the bird as it probed the earth with its beak.

"This is the Stewart Island brown kiwi," Steven said. "It's a young bird because it's not huge."

"I thought you were taking photos," Cullen whispered.

"Maybe the next one."

The kiwi continued feeding, seemingly not bothered by its human audience. Up this close, it was easy to hear the bird clearing its nostrils. It wandered beneath a bushy fern, disappearing. Anna signaled they were moving on again, and they could switch on their torches.

"That was amazing," Grace said.

"It was," Cullen agreed, squeezing her shoulder.

He meant every word, and the warm sensation she'd felt in her chest since they'd arrived in Stewart Island grew more prominent and tighter. Even though she'd hoped Jeff would enjoy Stewart Island and participate in the activities she'd wanted to try, she'd known booking here was a mistake. She'd made the reservation anyway, in the hope they'd discover more common ground. It wouldn't have worked. Looking back now, she could admit this truth. Cullen had made this holiday special, and it wasn't just the lovemaking. No matter what happened in the future, this was a time she'd remember until her dying day.

That she was falling for Cullen since he'd blasted aside her objections, she tried not to dwell on too much. The age difference...

Best she not count on this being a forever kind of relationship. She and Jeff had recently split, so she should take the time to find herself and to heal. A pang tightened her chest, and she rubbed the achy spot.

She stepped over a stick, her eyes suddenly stinging with unshed tears. That was the moment she admitted her error—this week, she'd toppled into love with Cullen.

Bad, bad mistake.

Jeff huddled in the Oban pub and grunted at the locals, who attempted to engage him in conversation. He yanked his cap over his head, hunched his shoulders, and willed time to pass. It was nine in the evening and too early to search the lodge on the hill. One positive thing about this place was that darkness fell earlier than in the north.

He watched the other customers but didn't see Grace with her new guy.

God, that pissed him off—that she'd bring another man on their honeymoon.

A snarl escaped him, the sound loud enough to draw curious glances from the couple at the next table. When he glowered at them, they averted their gazes, finished their drinks and left.

To pass the time, since he didn't want to start his search for another hour, he turned on his phone to check his messages. His phone beeped non-stop for a minute, and when he scanned the missed calls, his right hand trembled. Damn, he'd been afraid of that. He dragged in a breath and tapped the keys necessary to hear his messages.

"Where are you, Jeffie?" His boss's hoarse rumble had his gut churning. The sharp click indicating the end of the message had Jeff jumping.

The next message played. "Thought you had a few brains. You know this won't end well for you," Matthew snarled. "I want my product. You didn't strike me as a stupid fuck. Bring it to me by Saturday, and I'll go easier on you."

Jeff winced since it was Tuesday.

He listened to the rest of the messages and wondered if he should just grab a flight from Queenstown to Melbourne or Sydney and from there disappear into the crowds in the big city. Then his mind turned to Grace, and his back straightened. No way in hell did he intend to let her get away with making him look stupid.

Jeff checked the time and thrust his phone into his hoodie pocket. After draining the last of his beer, he stood.

The main street of Oban, such as it was, appeared empty. Jeff stood outside the pub, allowing his night vision to adjust to the scant light. While lights shone from the buildings near the pub and a few hillside homes, there were large expanses of land lying in darkness.

"Excellent," he muttered, heavy on the sarcasm, as he headed toward the place where Grace had chosen to stay. Once away from the pub, his vision became problematic. The footpath ended, and he almost face-planted when he failed to see a pothole in the middle of the road.

His arms windmilled, but he remained upright. "Bloody hick town."

Jeff limped a few steps, the twinge in his back telling him he'd tweaked an old injury. Would nothing go right this week? He pressed his hands into the small of his back and rubbed the achy spot.

A car crawled along the road, prompting Jeff to step behind the bus shelter. It drove past and turned down the next street, not far beyond the school. Jeff's breath eased out, and his racing heart slowed. This business was stressing the hell out of him.

He continued, sliding through the night and watching for anything or anyone that might cause him problems. At the base of the steep hill, he paused once again.

At this end of the town, the light was scant, and whenever the moon slipped behind the clouds, he blundered like a clumsy man. Finally, he drew his phone out of his pocket and switched on the flashlight app.

It was so quiet. Too quiet, the lack of noise giving him the heebie-jeebies. Give him a busy city with streetlights and masses of people and vehicles. This silence was plain creepy.

A thump from up ahead had him freezing, his pulse jumping like a startled rabbit. A cry escaped him, and the thump became a series of crashes as if something large loitered up ahead. He cursed under his breath, nervous sweat breaking out on his back and torso. What the hell?

He hesitated, every particle of him poised to retreat. *Idiot.* How would he get his hands on that bloody statue?

"Suck it up, Jeff." He took a deep breath and proceeded with caution.

The crashes sounded again, but they were retreating now. Some type of animal? He had no idea. As far as he knew, the island had little in the way of livestock. He stopped again to listen, and when he heard nothing out of place, he continued to slog his way up the hill.

Damn, what sort of moron built a place at the top of a hill like this?

If he owned the place, the first thing he'd do would be to put in a lift or cable car to get visitors to the peak of this dirt mound.

Each breath sawed in and out of his lungs. His legs ached. His back complained each step of the way, and he couldn't see worth a damn. Misery rode him, sweat trickling down his spine. He'd have to switch off his torch soon in case an eagle-eyed local spotted him.

Jeff kept plodding. One foot after the other, hunching his shoulders as he attempted to ignore the pain shooting along his limbs. Finally, *finally*, he reached the lodge where Grace was staying.

Jeff risked using his torch until he reached the safety of the wooden deck, otherwise he'd trip and likely—given his luck—break his neck.

He caught a floral scent and a trace of green in the air. The leaves in the trees rustled, and the moon peeked from behind a cloud for scant seconds, allowing him to orientate himself better. Ah!

A set of steps. He shone his torch in that direction, checked for witnesses, then traversed the steps as fast as his sore back allowed him.

Winded and hurting, he groaned under his breath and ducked into a deep shadow while he gasped through the darting pain in his back. Under normal circumstances, he would've flagged his mission and ordered one of his recruits to toss the rooms and search for his statue. Unfortunately, nothing about this mess was ordinary.

His temper flared, but he tried to tamp it down and focus. From memory, Grace and the neighbor had walked to the right once they hit the stairs, which meant he wouldn't need to check the rooms on his left. They'd been visible from where he'd stood, and he would've seen their destination. Right, it looked as if there were three rooms—no, four—to the right.

The first had the curtains tied back, and from what he could see, it was empty. Three left to check then. He tried the first door he reached. *Locked.* Jeff hesitated, wondering what to do next.

Perhaps he'd try the other doors. If he found one unlocked, he could enter, and it wouldn't take him long to rule out if it was Grace's. He'd know immediately because of her grandma clothes. It had been embarrassing taking her anywhere because she dressed years older than her age. The next door he attempted to open was also locked. *Bum.* He moved onto the last and found that one barred to him.

Jeff hesitated. The curtains were open, which told him no one was at home.

But which one was Grace's?

He checked the farthest away first and tried the door again before noticing the occupants hadn't closed the window properly. He inched it open before realizing he wouldn't gain access that way either since the window had a security latch. Jeff bared his teeth and glared at the door, wishing he'd grabbed a set of tools to help him gain admittance. He ignored the sweat running down his forehead and glanced over his shoulder to check for witnesses.

He was alone.

Jeff sucked in a breath and removed his hoodie. He bundled it up and twisted it around his wrist. A second later, he punched the glass door. It smashed with the force of his blow, and Jeff's heart beat faster. Seconds later, he stood inside, the broken glass crunching beneath his shoes. He switched on the light, then hurriedly yanked the curtains across the window. A quick search later revealed this was not Grace's room. It looked as if two men shared this space. His lip twisted as he studied the king bed. Queers.

Jeff shook his hoodie free of glass and stepped onto the deck. The last thing he did was switch off the light. For an instant, he was blind, and the moon disappearing behind the clouds didn't help. He cursed under his breath but used the subdued outdoor lighting to guide him to the next without tripping over the patio furniture.

Once again, he scanned the vicinity, and not a person or creature stirred. He protected his fist with his hoodie and smashed his way through the door to gain entrance. A quick search of the clothes revealed this one didn't belong to Grace either. Oh, it was tidy enough to belong to her, but the clothes were way too modern.

He'd just smashed the window of the third room when someone shouted.

"Hey! What the devil are you doing?" A man appeared at the end of the deck, his face pale in the night. "Carol, call the police!"

Jeff's heart knocked against his ribs, his legs threatening to fail and toss him on his arse. He barreled along the deck, heading straight for a skinny woman who was blocking his escape. Leading with his shoulder, he ran straight at her. She side-stepped and stuck out her foot, the action so fast, Jeff couldn't keep his feet. He flew forward but caught his weight with his forearms.

Panic and fear had him staggering to his feet and half running and limping into the darkness. He sped around the curve in the road, but instead of fleeing down the steep hill, he ducked behind a bush and made himself as small as possible. Not a moment too soon, either.

Footsteps thudded after him.

"Can you see him?" a man asked.

"No," a woman replied. "I'll call the manager."

A few seconds later, Jeff heard her speaking to someone on her phone.

Jeff's breaths came in noisy gasps, and he covered his mouth with his hand to minimize the noise. The last thing he wanted was for them to catch him and cart him off. That would magnify his problems.

One—the cops might fingerprint him and discover that Jeffrey Howard wasn't his actual name. And two—if the cops got their hands on him, Matthew would learn of his capture because he had contacts everywhere.

That would make it easy for Matthew to get to him. His life wouldn't be worth crap.

Damn, Grace Feeney.

17

BREAK IN

CULLEN SPOTTED THE COP car and its flashing lights as they reached the summit. He stopped, his gut telling him to survey the vicinity. He'd learned to trust his instincts.

"What is it?" Grace whispered, obeying his silent command to halt.

"Not sure. Can you see anything out of place?"

"No, but it's weird. I'd swear someone was watching us."

"Yeah," Cullen agreed. "Let's hustle. It's safer nearer the cop in the light."

Susan, the lodge manager, was speaking with the cop and spotted them first. She smiled, but it was clear her hostess duties were automatic and her smile ragged at the edges. "Ah, you're back from kiwi spotting. How was it?"

"It was brilliant," Grace said, answering for both of them. "We saw six different kiwis tonight. The guide said it was a lucky group. It was… Words can't describe how wonderful seeing a kiwi in the wild is—so unique."

"I'm glad." Susan smiled again, but now they were closer, it was easy to see the strain in her features and her clenched fingers. "Unfortunately, we've had trouble here tonight. Someone—a man—broke into three of the rooms. One of them was yours. Can you go with Bryan, our local cop, and let him know if anything is missing?"

Cullen shared a glance with Grace.

"It was a man?" he asked.

"Yes, two of the guests arrived back from a different kiwi excursion. The man smashed their window as they stepped onto the deck."

"Do we have a description?" Cullen asked.

"Close to six feet in height. Possibly blond hair but they can't be certain. He was wearing dark clothes. They only glimpsed him for a moment."

Cullen caught Grace's frown, and it was apparent their minds ran in tandem. Cullen squeezed her hand, and she pressed her lips together. It might be better if they waited until they had the cop alone before they spoke about Jeff.

"Can we check our room?" Grace asked.

"Sure," Bryan said. He was much shorter than Cullen and close to fifty, but the gray-haired man moved with ease and appeared fit. Cullen noted the way Bryan's gaze swept the area and approved. This man knew what he was doing, and despite being a cop in a small town where they probably had little trouble, he took his job seriously.

The cop led the way along the deck. Their room was the middle one of the three at the end. "Watch out for the glass.

It's all over the floor. Can you take a quick look and tell me if anything is missing?"

"I had my camera and wallet with me. Hopefully, my tablet is still in the bedside drawer," Grace said.

Cullen had left nothing valuable but scanned the drawers' contents beside the bed before doing a rapid walk-through the rest of their room. He returned to speak to the police officer. "I can't see anything out of place or missing."

Grace came to join them, her cute nose wrinkled in a frown. "Nothing of mine is missing."

"Right. Neither of you has seen anyone skulking around the place?" the cop asked.

Grace exchanged a glance with him, and Cullen answered for both of them.

"No," he said. "We've been in and out while trying to see as much of Stewart Island as possible."

"Understandable," the cop said. "If you see anything or remember something, let me know."

"Sure," Cullen said.

Grace gestured at their room floor. "Can we clean up the glass now?"

The cop removed his camera from the bag he carried. "I'll take photos first."

"No, you're not cleaning up," Susan stated from behind them. She handed over a bottle of wine. "It's a lovely evening now that the wind has dropped. Why don't you sit out here while I sort out this mess?"

"We don't mind helping."

"No, I won't hear of it," the woman said. "If you'd prefer

a cup of tea, I can bring you a pot."

"A glass of wine sounds lovely," Cullen said because it was obvious Susan was in shock and rattled by the break-in. This was her way of regaining control.

"I'll be right back with snacks to go with that drink." She disappeared before anyone could object.

"This is Susan's way of making sure her guests are okay," the cop said, confirming Cullen's theory. "Best to roll with it until she regains her equilibrium."

Cullen took Grace's hand and led her outside. They chose seats at an out-of-the-way table, and Cullen dragged their chairs close together.

"You okay?" In the dim light, he surveyed her features.

Grace frowned and leaned closer. "Do you think it's Jeff?"

"The turd? Why would he do something like that?"

"Maybe the statue he keeps harping on about? We didn't check it too closely," Grace murmured. "I mean, it looked ordinary to me, but what if there is something inside it?"

"I meant to break it open, but you distracted me." He placed a kiss on the tip of her nose. "We'll check it out once we can get back in our room. We might as well have a glass of this lovely red wine and chill. Are you tired?"

"No, not really. I'm too excited to sleep."

"Excellent." Cullen cupped her face and gave in to his urge to kiss her properly. This woman made his thoughts turn to his future. Maybe he should think harder on Josh's proposition to look after his security business when Ash needed Josh's help with diplomatic functions and the like.

Cullen pulled back, trying to keep the kiss from escalating into something unfit for outside the bedroom.

With regret, he stepped away and opened the bottle of pinot. It was a rich, ruby red as he poured the wine into the two glasses. He handed a glass to Grace and picked up his to offer a toast. "To friends and lovers," he said.

Grace grinned. "Friends and lovers." She drank and issued an appreciative sigh. "This is delicious." She set down her glass, her expression slipping into a frown. "We think Jeff was into drugs, right?"

"The clues point that way," Cullen agreed.

"What do we do if we find drugs inside the statue?"

"We need to make sure it's still where I left it first," Cullen cautioned. "We look once it's safe, and if we find anything suspicious, we'll go to the local cop with what we have. He'll know what to do."

"But if Jeff is here—"

"Remember, you promised not to speak of the idiot. I have other things I'd prefer to discuss with you."

"Like what?"

Cullen glanced over his shoulder and sipped his wine while he waited for the cop to move on to one of the other rooms. Once they were alone again, he placed his glass on the table and took Grace's from her too. He scooped her off her chair and plopped her on his knee, grinning at her feminine *eep* of surprise. Cullen wrapped his arms around her and claimed her mouth, showing her with actions rather than words how he'd prefer to spend his time. She softened, leaning into him and chasing his lips when he would've spoken again.

"Like a night of hot sex," he said once he'd lifted his head.

"It's morning. It has to be because it was eleven-thirty when we left the boat at the jetty."

Cullen waggled his eyebrows at Grace. "Even better. Morning sex."

"*Pfff*," Grace said, but she was laughing. "I'm going to need a holiday when we get home to rest up."

"I was hoping there would be lots of resting together," Cullen said, watchful when her smile faded. "Our friendship won't end once we arrive home or when I get back from my next furlough. Beautiful, Grace, if that's where your mind is going, you need to do a U-turn. I'm serious about you. I've told you that before, but I guess after the douchebag, it's hard to get your head straight. That kind of thing can rattle a woman and create turmoil with her commonsense."

Grace's mouth fell open, and she resembled a cute urchin. She poked him in the chest. "Are you telling me I'm a nutcase?"

"If you're thinking about throwing something perfect like our relationship away, then yes. That makes you silly. Do you know how many people find the one who completes them and fills their angst with calmness? Not many. That's why divorce rates are so high. Men and women keep trying because they know the gold at the end of the rainbow is worth it."

Her eyes grew enormous and round, and her mouth had fallen open again. He didn't warn her if she kept this up, he might give her a new nickname—goldfish. Goldie for short.

"You really think we're that suited for each other? The years between us don't bother you?"

"Have you ever known me to lie to you, cupcake?"

"You've always been truthful. I remember when I was babysitting you, and my boyfriend came to visit. You told me he was a waste of my time." She grinned at the memory.

"You were angry when I said it," Cullen said with caution.

"Why *did* you say that? Most kids of your age wouldn't have commented. They would've hidden in their room or watched television or played X-Box."

"I liked you then. You differed from the other babysitters Mum arranged for us."

"Oh."

They stared at each other for a long moment, and Cullen's heart did a weird jig against his chest. "I like you a lot, Grace. I always have. Please give us a chance, and don't worry about other people's opinions or what the dick told you."

"Okay," she said. "I can do that since I return the sentiment. These few days have been so much fun. We enjoy the same things, and I've never had that with another man. Plus, you encourage me in my baking, and you don't tell me I'm wasting my time. You're my champion."

"I am," he agreed, and because he couldn't help it, he cupped her face in his hands and kissed her again. The kiss started gently, but he tried to put everything in his heart into the interaction. The more time he spent with Grace, the more confident he was of what he wanted for his future.

Grace.

While she might have doubts—hell, she kept bringing them up and placing roadblocks where none existed—he had none.

Grace pulled back, her luscious breasts rising and falling rapidly. "I'm not sure what you're doing to me, Cullen Turner," she murmured, her voice trembling. "I can't concentrate when you kiss me, touch me. It's like my brain packs up and goes on holiday."

"Mine too," Cullen replied. "But I'm embracing the magic between us. I want what my friends have with their wives. I want more than this week, but I've told you that already."

"Okay."

"You said that before," Cullen said, this time with a bite in his words. He was a military man, used to following orders and making decisions on his own whenever necessary. "I won't change my mind, cupcake. Now kiss me again, then we'll watch the stars together and finish this delightful wine."

In answer, Grace initiated their next kiss, her soft lips pressing against his. Immediately, the tension generated by the repeated discussion of their relationship faded. His heart beat faster, and he groaned against her mouth. His last remaining thought before he lost himself in her was that for this to end would be a crime.

Grace clung to Cullen, so happy she wondered if her heart might burst.

"Uh-hum." A cough accompanied the non-committal

sound.

Grace gasped against Cullen's lips, and heat rushed to her cheeks. Cullen didn't seem to harbor the same discomfort and merely gave her a quick peck on the mouth and loosened his hold enough for them to both glance in Susan's direction.

"I'm sorry for the interruption," she said. "The glass is cleared away, and I've placed a temporary board across the hole. I'll get my handyman to make the repairs tomorrow. That's if I can get replacement glass from Invercargill."

Grace smiled at the woman. "It won't matter if the glass takes a few days. Cullen and I realize none of this is your fault."

Susan dipped her head in acknowledgment. "I've left the door shut, but it's not locked. Good night," she added hurriedly as two people walked up the stairs at the far end of the deck. She rushed over to them and spoke in a quiet voice.

"This break-in has distressed her," Cullen said.

"I'm not surprised. The crime rate is low here." She started to scramble off Cullen's lap, but he tightened his grip around her waist. "There is a perfectly good seat over there."

"I like touching you," he stated in a voice that suggested her arguments would lead nowhere. "This way is perfectly comfortable."

Grace gave in and reached for her glass of wine. She took a sip, savoring the fruity taste across her taste buds. "This wine is delicious."

Cullen picked up his glass and drank. "As soon as we're

finished here, we'll get the statue and scrutinize it more closely. You keep distracting me."

"Me?"

"Yes, you with your sexy curves and gorgeous smile."

"You really think there is something hinky about the statue?"

"This break-in is making my spidey senses tingle. I've learned not to ignore my gut. Every time I do, things haven't gone well."

"Let's go now. We might as well take our wine with us."

"All right," he agreed.

Cullen helped her to balance until she stood on her feet. Once he rose, she picked up her glass and followed Cullen into their room.

True to her word, the manager had cleared the mess, and apart from the board across the door, they'd never have known anything was amiss.

Cullen drew the curtains, taking extra care to ensure there were no gaps for anyone to peek. She understood what he was doing without asking.

"Is someone spying on us?"

"Yes," Cullen said.

"I sensed eyes on us, but I told myself it was my imagination."

"No, someone was watching. They kept out of sight, but they were there." He hesitated. "I should investigate."

"No," Grace said. "We should check out the gnome doing the one-finger salute. Did you put it back in my bag? I'll get it."

"No, I'll come with you, and we'll open it in the walk-in

wardrobe. Let me lock the door."

Grace entered the area and flicked on the light. She dragged out her bag and unzipped the side pocket where she'd stashed the gnome. Its snooty expression always raised a smile, but this time, she scanned it with closer scrutiny. She turned the statue over and was studying it from all angles when Cullen joined her.

"I can't see anything strange about it. There aren't any seams."

"No," Cullen agreed. "I didn't see any join. We'll have to smash it."

"Wait. I quite like it. I don't like the idea of destroying it." She shook the gnome and set it down on a wardrobe shelf. "If there is something inside the statue, it's not rattling around."

"Perhaps we can break the bottom," Cullen suggested. "Let me grab my knife to break it open."

"Are you sure we have to damage it?"

"Why would the dipstick want this statue back?"

Grace shrugged. "You're right. Initially, I took it because it seemed appropriate payback. A way of giving him the finger."

Cullen grinned. "Understandable, although I would've flattened his nose." He disappeared and reappeared with a knife.

"Where did that come from?"

"My bag," he said. "But I always sleep with it within reach. This knife has saved my life a time or two."

Grace suppressed her shudder and fought to keep her face impassive. While intellectually she understood

Cullen's army job placed him in danger, she'd tried not to dwell on it. That had been easier when she hadn't known how it felt to kiss him.

Cullen used the knife hilt to give the base of the gnome a sharp tap. The statue split in half, spilling bags of white pills across the floor. Grace gaped at the contents.

"Drugs," Cullen said. "Ecstasy, probably."

"In my house," Grace said in a faint voice. "This was going on under my nose. I've been so stupid."

"This isn't your fault. You have a kind heart, and the moron took advantage of your good nature."

"What are we going to do now?"

"Right now, I'm going to hide everything in a bag. In the morning, we'll visit the local cop and hand everything over to him."

Grace stooped to pick up the packets.

"No," Cullen said in a sharp voice. "We don't want our fingerprints on the packets. A precaution."

"How will you pick them up, then?"

Cullen retreated and returned seconds later with a handful of tissues and the plastic bag that had formerly held a pair of his shoes. "This should do the trick."

18

ON THE TRAIL

GRACE STEPPED BACK TO get out of the way, allowing Cullen to take charge. The truth—his presence soothed her shock. She would've panicked and picked up the packets. She might've flushed them down the loo or done something similar instead of taking them to the local policeman.

"Do you think Jeff wants his drugs back?"

"I'd lay a bet on it," Cullen said.

"What are you going to do with them overnight?"

"I'll put them back in the wardrobe behind my stack of shirts," Cullen said. "Anyone coming after them will need to get past me. I'm a light sleeper and will wake if anyone comes into our room. They'll need to struggle past the locked door and the curtains before they get to us."

"That is so reassuring," Grace said, not holding back on her sarcasm.

A laugh burst from Cullen, and he was still chuckling when he entered the walk-in wardrobe to hide the contraband.

Grace yawned. It'd been a long but eventful day, and she needed to sleep if they were to go jet-boating up the river. She sat on the bed to remove her walking shoes.

"You tired?" Cullen asked.

"Why?"

"It's late, and we have an early start."

Grace sighed and pushed to her feet. "True. We've had an eventful day."

"I wanted to make love to you again," Cullen said, his eyes searching her face.

Grace's gaze jumped to his, and he stepped closer, his hands cupping her shoulders.

"But holding you will work for now," he whispered against her neck.

"We still have four days here."

She turned in his arms to study his expression. He meant every word. Jeff would've railed and whined and snapped at her if she'd told him no.

"I'm tired too," Cullen admitted. "But since I've shared a bed with you, I've slept better than I have in months."

Grace stood on tiptoes and pressed her mouth against his. "That's great," she said once she pulled back.

"Let's go to bed," Cullen said and tugged his T-shirt over his head.

Grace stared at the broad expanse of male chest. The sleek muscles made her mouth water, and her fingers itch to touch. In a few moments, he'd cuddle her against all that masculine goodness. The happy thought let her slough off her anxiety over the drugs they'd found in the statue. She hated that Jeff had tricked her. His stealing from her was bad enough, but that the horrid man had used her money to purchase drugs pricked her anger. If she ever saw that ratbag again, she'd punch him in his imperious nose.

"Are you going to stand there all night, staring at me?"

Grace winked at Cullen. "There are worse sights."

He laughed again, and naked, climbed into bed. He dragged the covers to his waist and propped his hands behind his head, his gaze bright. "My turn now."

Grace groaned but knew better than to complain of her weight or anything else Cullen might construe as lack of confidence. She shed her jeans, her fleece jacket, and the T-shirt she wore beneath. She'd already learned that Cullen loved her breasts. Best to flash those and distract him while she found her nightie.

"Naked," he ordered. "Please," he added, softening his abrupt tone.

Shaking her head, she discarded her underwear and hurriedly climbed into the bed. Cullen dragged her into his arms, his body heat making her cozy in no time. He placed a kiss on her shoulder, her neck, before reaching over to tap the bedside lamp controls on her side of the bed.

"Cupcake, I love having you in my arms. When we get home, I'll stay with you. That way, we can keep an eye on any unwelcome visitors, and I can rip into my home renovations."

"My house won't feel safe," Grace murmured. It had

always been her haven, but now Jeff had spoiled that.

"My friend, Josh, works in security and installs alarms. We'll put in an alarm and take a few other precautions. Honestly, once the local buyers learn the dick is no longer there, they'll stop coming around."

"I hope so. I don't know how I missed the strangers around the place."

Cullen resettled, his hands on her body sending a surge of warm prickles to life. "Everything will be fine. Go to sleep, and we'll deal with our problems tomorrow. Don't worry. We're not in any danger."

JEFF SAT IN THE shadows of the bush, rage pounding through his brain. *Bang. Bang. Bang.* The dull thud echoed in his ears until he wanted to scream. His pulse raced, and he ached to hurt someone, to see the drip of blood. His fingers curled as he imagined punching that dude with Grace. He wouldn't mind slapping Grace either.

God, that couple had appeared from nowhere. He hadn't heard them as he'd been about to break into the third room, confident it'd been the one he'd wanted.

He'd been wrong.

He'd discovered that once the cop had arrived. From his position, he hadn't been able to see anything, but sound carried, and his mistake had soon become clear. Grace's room was the first one he'd broken into and discarded as not right. He cursed under his breath as he wondered what the hell he was going to do next.

What if she didn't have the gnome statue?

No. No, he was confident she had it because the tape on the camera had shown her holding the statues. She and the man had discussed them. She'd placed three in the bag she'd later tossed on the sidewalk. The fourth, he couldn't say for certain because masculine broad shoulders had blocked the camera angle. The thought kept firing through his mind, but he kept coming back to the fact it hadn't been with the others, and the gnome giving the royal salute had always amused her. Didn't serial killers keep mementos of their crimes? This wasn't much different.

Jeff listened to the surrounding sounds and heard a morepork call and the chirp of crickets. The lights from the lodge above him blinked out one by one until only the security lights provided vision.

He stood and staggered a few steps before the blood flowed back into his cramped limbs. His gun pushed heavy against the small of his back and offered a sense of security.

A solution popped into his mind, and he stomped back up the road to the lodge. Rage propelled him closer, an adrenaline surge buzzing in his ears. His gaze zapped to the room where Grace and that man were probably fucking right now. Quick steps led him toward the room, and it was like walking through a tunnel.

He pulled out his gun and kicked in the door, guided to the weakness by the board on the broken window. It took him longer than he wanted—extended moments where his heart pounded so loud he couldn't hear his thoughts.

The light came on instantly. A man's low warning voice.

Jeff blinked, blinded by the light for precious seconds. When he refocused, he saw a tousled Grace, frantically trying to pull on clothes. Snarling, he raised his gun and pointed it at her. Without a second thought, he fired. Grace released a shriek of pain and fell to the ground.

"Grace!" the man shouted, freezing when Jeff swiveled to point the gun at him.

"Where is my statue?"

"We don't have it," the man said.

"Don't lie to me," Jeff snapped. He glanced at Grace and could only see her leg. "Grace! Answer me, dammit. I know you have the gnome, and I want it back. I'll shoot you again."

Jeff caught a flash of movement from the corner of his eye. He whirled, but the man was on him. He was bigger and more solid than Jeff had realized. The man punched him, and Jeff's head jerked back. He saw stars, and when the man hit him again, he lost his grip on the gun.

"Grace, stay back," the man warned.

"Take this, you ratfink bastard," Grace shrieked.

A blink later, something thumped over the back of Jeff's head. He crumpled, and everything went black as he struck the ground. He must've only lost consciousness for brief seconds, but when he came to, the man was on him and busy tying Jeff's hands together. Jeff struggled and discovered his bound legs. He could do nothing more than wriggle.

"Grace, you're bleeding."

"The bullet grazed my arm. I didn't realize it'd hurt so

much. No, that was stupid. Of course, a gunshot hurts." She visibly trembled. "I'm lucky he didn't kill me."

"If you had given me back my statue, I wouldn't need to be here, but you ruined everything."

Grace stomped over to Jeff, her face a mask of anger and something Jeff had never seen before.

"You shouldn't have come home early," Jeff snapped.

"You pompous oaf." She darted closer and kicked him in the ribs. "Jerk! None of this is my fault. All I did was give you my trust. You were the one who stole my money and sold drugs from my house. You slept with Julia in my bed."

"We had a good thing going," Jeff said.

"Stop talking," Grace snapped and kicked him again.

"Stop kicking me," Jeff snarled.

"I'd kick you harder if I had shoes on," she said with unwarranted relish.

Jeff's ribs ached enough as it was, and the guy who had jumped him had landed one or two stinging blows. Not that he would voice this fact.

"I'll find something to gag him with," the man said. "Can you ring the cop?"

A siren sounded in the distance.

"It sounds as if someone has already done that," Grace said.

"Bitch," Jeff snarled seconds before the man slapped something across his mouth.

Grace glared at him, but Jeff ignored her while he attempted to free his arms. The idiots hadn't searched him, and he had a knife too.

19

CALLING THE COPS

GRACE SCOOPED UP HER clothes and rushed into the bathroom. Before dressing, she studied her arm and noted blood had run down her biceps to her elbow. She grabbed a flannel and carefully cleaned the wound. Thankfully, when she lifted the flannel, she saw the injury wasn't as bad as she'd suspected. She grabbed a handful of tissues and made a pad to press against her arm. The wad remained white, the blood flow sluggish, and relief flooded her. She wouldn't need to see a doctor unless the wound became infected.

Grace muttered under her breath while she dressed. Jeff was an idiot, and she wished she'd kicked him harder. She pulled on a shirt and rapidly fastened the buttons. As soon as she was decent, she hustled back to Cullen. Jeff wriggled on the floor like the worm he was while Cullen eyed him in disgust.

The siren continued coming closer until it abruptly cut off.

Grace thrust her feet into her runners and stalked to the door. She pulled the curtain back and stepped onto the deck. Susan hovered near the breakfast room, and minutes later, the cop appeared.

"Are you all right?" Susan wrung her hands.

"A man broke into our room," Grace said in an understatement.

Cullen came to stand beside Grace.

"Where's the man?" the cop asked, eyes watchful.

"He's tied up—" Grace replied before someone grasped her arm and a knife blade at her throat had her head jerking back.

"Stand back," Jeff snarled.

Cullen cursed, loud enough for Grace to hear. Then Jeff was dragging her away from Cullen.

"Stand back," he snarled. "Where is my statue?"

Grace laughed, an edge of hysteria lacing the bark of sound. "You're crazy. Even if I had your statue, which I don't, how will you escape the island? The only way off is via ferry or flying. Both places will watch for you. There is no escape."

"It's your fault, you bitch."

The pressure around her neck tightened, and her arm throbbed and ached. It had bled again, and instead of feeling fear, fury pumped through her. Jeff was an idiot. A moron. Despite the way he held her so tight, she forced herself to relax. She ignored the knife at her throat. She didn't think he'd hurt her—at least, not until he had possession of the gnome.

"How do you know I have the gnome?" she asked.

Jeff's grip tightened. "I knew you had it. I want it back."

"All right," Grace said. "Why do you want it?"

"That's for me to know," Jeff snapped. "Where is it?"

"You'll need to let me go so I can get it for you."

"Stay away from us," Jeff warned. "If you don't, I'll slit her throat."

"Don't give it to him, cupcake." Cullen's expression was warrior-scary, but stress showed too. He hated this situation and probably blamed himself.

That made two of them.

"Let her go," the cop said in a calm voice. "She's right. You can't escape. Let her go, and we can discuss this."

"I'm not stupid," Jeff said with a sneer. "The moment I release her, you'll be all over me. Grace is my ticket out of here."

Not if she could help it. But what to do? She glanced at Cullen and saw his face had whitened with strain. He *was* blaming himself for her predicament. Not his fault. She'd tell him that as soon as she had the opportunity. But right now, she could do with a plan. Maybe keep him talking. "Jeff!"

His body jolted at her sharp tone, and she felt the bite of the knife at her neck.

"If you let me go, I'll take you to the statue."

Jeff didn't move. "Where?"

"It's in the wardrobe."

"Where?" He glanced around the bedroom. "There's no wardrobe here."

"It's a walk-in one. Just past the bed, there's a fridge and tea-making facility. If you walk that far, you'll see the walk-in wardrobe beyond that."

"Show me," Jeff demanded.

He was an idiot if he thought he'd get past Cullen and the cop with his stupid drugs.

"I can't see where I'm walking with the knife at my throat," Grace complained. Her heart pumped faster than usual, but anger bolstered her courage. The urge to box his ears was intense. A plan slid into place. She'd have one chance to escape. One opportunity to give Cullen an opening to overpower the jerk. "Jeff, move the knife, or you'll kill me before I can tell you the statue's location."

"You've told me it's in the wardrobe."

No mistaking that smug attitude. She'd enjoy taking Jeff down a peg or two. The man had not a jot of respect for her. She only wished she'd realized that earlier. "You think I'd hide your drugs in plain sight."

"What?" He'd lowered the knife to dig into her ribs and now slid a glance at the cop.

Grace lurched forward abruptly, jerking from Jeff's touch. At the same time, she bent her right knee and thrust it backward and up. Jeff howled on contact, crumpling to hold his groin.

Cullen and the cop were on him in a heartbeat while Grace grabbed the clean tea towel and held it to her throat. It came away bloody but not as bad as she feared. She stalked back out to the main bedroom and found Jeff cuffed on the floor and still whining. His head turned in her direction, and he let out a snarl.

"I want her charged with assault," he spat at the cop.

"You held her at knifepoint," the cop countered, his gaze hard. "I saw you threaten her. Would you mind helping me get him back to the station?" he asked Cullen. "I can drop you back here once he's locked away. I'll get him transferred to Invercargill tomorrow morning."

Cullen turned to Grace. "Are you okay? How is your neck?"

She crossed the distance between them and lifted the tea towel. "I'll live. The cut isn't deep." She turned back to the cop. "He stole money from me and ran a tinny house from my premises without my knowledge. I want him charged with that."

"I'll get the drugs we found. You'll want those as evidence," Cullen said.

"Help me get him to the vehicle first," the cop said.

Grace followed them outside.

"Drugs? What are you talking about?" Jeff shouted. "I don't have any drugs. All I wanted was the return of my statue."

"You are such a liar," Grace said. "I don't know what I ever saw in you. You're a whining dick, and you need to grow a pair."

"That man will give you the flick. He's using you," Jeff shouted.

"Cullen isn't like you."

"Let me look at your neck," Susan said, halting Grace's tirade.

"It's not bad." Grace lifted the towel.

"He'll leave you," Jeff screamed.

Grace glanced up in time to see Cullen punch him. The man dropped, and Cullen and the cop hauled Jeff to the car.

Once they'd secured him inside, Cullen jogged up onto the deck. He disappeared into their room and reappeared carrying the bag of drugs.

"I won't be long," he promised and gave her a quick kiss before joining the local cop.

"It's not usually like this on the island," Susan said. "We get a few drunks and stupid holidaymakers from the mainland, but that's it. Nothing like this." She glanced along the deck at the damage to Grace's and Cullen's room. "I won't be able to get your door fixed until tomorrow, and I don't have a spare room for you right now." The woman's eyes glistened with unshed tears. "It-it's never, ever been like this before."

"The trouble followed me from Auckland. Honestly, it's no problem," Grace said. "Why don't we sweep up the glass and clear the worst of the damage? It's almost morning, anyway."

"Thank you for being so understanding," Susan said. "Most people would shout at me."

"Cullen and I are fine. Apart from this drama, we've loved every minute of our visit."

"Let me clean your neck with an antiseptic. Then, I'll go into clean-up mode."

Grace sent Susan a reassuring smile because it was obvious the burden of responsibility weighed heavily on her shoulders tonight. "None of this is your doing. You can lay the blame squarely on me. Jeff's arrival is my fault."

Susan's eyes narrowed. "How do you know this man?"

Grace hesitated over what to tell the woman and settled for simplicity. "We were friends once." It was none of her business that Grace had come on her honeymoon with another man. A trade that worked for Grace, for sure. Cullen was... He was... Mere words couldn't describe Cullen. He was solid and rugged, yet with her, he was gentle and loving. He made her feel better about herself. He was everything. "Jeff followed me from Auckland."

"He is not a nice man." The inflection said everything. Susan doubted Grace's judgment when it came to men.

"I agree." Grace wanted to defend herself but bit back the instinct to explain further. "I hope the authorities lock him up for a long time."

"There." Susan patted the cut on Grace's throat with the cotton wool ball. "The bleeding has stopped. You were lucky."

"Believe me, I know," Grace replied. "Let me help you sweep up the glass."

"No, I couldn't—"

"I insist," Grace said. "At least that way, we might get a little sleep tonight."

The woman glanced at her wristwatch. "It's almost five. I usually get up at six to prepare everything for breakfast. One couple is leaving this morning. Once I clean their room, you can shift accommodation."

"That's unnecessary," Grace said.

"I'll need to order replacement glass and the door frame from Invercargill. We have a retired builder who will install the frame and windows for me, but I suspect the stock will take a few days. You can't stay in a room that exposes you to the elements."

"Thank you," Grace said. "Ah, that sounds like a vehicle now. Hopefully, it's Cullen."

Grace guessed right, as seconds later, Cullen jogged up the steps and stalked over to her. He tilted her head up to study the marks Jeff had inflicted.

"It doesn't look too bad, cupcake."

"No."

He jerked her from the chair and wrapped his arms around her in a breath-stealing hug. "I should paddle your backside for your little performance earlier," he whispered against her ear.

"I had to do something." His warm breath had the usual effect on her, pushing her pulse into a speedier beat and darting awareness of his size and masculinity through her. Now, she had a reel of images to go with her imagination and desire pulsed to life in her.

"Not at the risk of your life, cupcake." He shuddered. "I don't want to imagine a world without you in it."

She burrowed even closer, savoring the way she felt in his arms.

Protected. Loved.

This last descriptive had her thoughts racing to a screeching halt. Despite Cullen's protestations and his assurances that they made a great couple, the tiny snake of distrust and disbelief wormed into her brain. Those doubt-demons rode her subconscious, flinging out waves of unease and anxiety.

She kept them to herself because Cullen believed they

had a future.

Her—she'd decided to live each day one at a time. It was the best thing to do. Either way, she suspected forthcoming heartbreak, but instead of worrying about it, Grace shoved the notion from her head and focused on Cullen and everything good in her world.

The cops had Jeff in custody.

"The local cop wants us to give him an official statement later today. I told him we could meet him mid-morning."

Grace stepped back, but Cullen didn't loosen his embrace much. She sent him a quizzical glance.

"You could've died," he said. "I've never felt so terrified."

"Jeff is in custody now," she murmured, her chest aching with the wave of adoration and happiness all wrapped up with a bow of regret. "Let's shove him from our minds and enjoy the rest of our holiday."

Cullen's smile was dazzling bright, and her heart squeezed with longing. "I can get on board with that."

Grace, seeking to lighten her mood, winked at him. "Perhaps we could have an afternoon nap since there is no point going back to bed. It's almost morning."

"Sounds like a plan," Cullen agreed. "We should have a snooze every day."

If only, Grace thought, even as she returned his smile with a broad one of her own. She could do with more images for her Cullen reel before he left again.

20

HOME AGAIN

"I'LL CALL JOSH AS soon as we land," Cullen said.

"To check on my house?" The flight back to Auckland had been bittersweet and non-eventful. Back to normal. Back to work. *Back to reality.*

"Yes. Josh installed cameras for me and did a drive past each day."

"That was nice of him."

"I've done the odd favor for him. It's what mates do."

"You're lucky to have wonderful friends. It sounds sad, but most of mine have either moved away from Auckland or given up trying to meet with me. My hours are crazy sometimes."

"Have you thought about getting a new job?" Cullen asked. "Or you could try to get your idea for online cakes started."

"Jeff stole my savings. I can't do anything until I get

a backstop behind me. Most catering businesses fail in the first six months of opening. Usually, it's because the owners tried to move too fast or go too big straightaway. I don't want to end up a statistic."

"What about if you went on a smaller scale? Did kids' lunchbox meals for busy parents? Or baked brownies for afternoon teas or special occasions? Or did dessert food boxes? You're probably too late for Christmas or New Year's marketing, but Valentine's Day is soon. Experiment a little and do romantic dessert boxes. Tell your boss you need two days off a week and use that time to prep."

Grace pondered dessert boxes for Valentine's Day. "That's a fantastic idea. Use the romantic day as a test of the market. I'd prefer to go with my strengths, which are baking and desserts. I could advertise on social media and keep the operation small."

"There you go," Cullen said.

The plane landed, and everyone collected their belongings and exited the domestic flight. While they waited for their luggage, Cullen rang Josh.

Grace spied their bags and grabbed them off the conveyor.

"I'll help," Cullen was saying when she returned to his side with both bags. "Sure. Tomorrow morning at six. No problem. No, stop apologizing. Ash is right. You need to rest that arm." He hung up.

"Is something wrong?"

"Josh broke his arm playing touch football with our friends. He has a big contract, and he asked if I was available to help."

"What about your renovations?"

"They'll keep," Cullen said. "I don't mind helping Josh until I have to return to the army."

The drive from the airport to Papakura didn't take long, and Grace's feel-good mood dispersed during the journey home. She had to work tomorrow, and Cullen did too. She guessed she'd see him a little, but the two months left of his break would pass swiftly.

Cullen pulled into his driveway.

"I guess I'd better start the laundry," Grace said, opening the door to exit Cullen's vehicle.

"Want Thai takeaway for dinner?"

One last meal together. She seized the opportunity to spend more time with Cullen. "Yes."

"Do you want anything in particular?"

"Surprise me," she said. "As long as it's not too spicy."

Cullen nodded. "I'll give you a buzz once I've placed the order. I'll do that in about an hour."

Grace nodded and retrieved her bag once Cullen had opened the rear. She took two steps before Cullen's big hand curled around her right shoulder.

"Don't I get a kiss?"

Grace whirled to face him, her quick move making him release his grip. She studied his face and couldn't read his expression. It wasn't open as it had been during their time in Stewart Island.

Before she replied, he closed the distance between them and kissed her hard. Once she responded to him, he gentled the contact, taking the kiss into seductive territory. She moaned against his mouth.

"That's better." He tucked a lock of hair behind Grace's ear and then stepped back. "I'll call you."

She nodded and plucked the keys from her pocket. Once inside, she dumped her bag and did a quick walk-through to ensure everything was in order with her house. It was, and she breathed a sigh of relief.

Time for laundry.

It was closer to two hours before Cullen rang her to say the food was on its way and she should come over to his place.

Grace had taken the time to shower and put on a pretty floral sundress, another of her new outfits. A sense of letdown bombarded her as she crossed the expanse of lawn to the gate between their two properties. Once they returned to work—tomorrow—everything would change. Revert to normal. She kept telling herself to enjoy the evening ahead, savor the time she had with Cullen. Although he'd told her he wanted her and showed he desired a future, the self-doubt wouldn't let go, digging in claws deep enough to cause her anxiety.

Grace halted at the wooden gate. "This negative Nelly attitude has got to stop." Above all, Cullen was her friend. She needed an attitude change because Cullen would soon tire of building up her confidence. She would if she were him. Even before Jeff, she'd had crises of self-confidence, all a legacy of her teen years.

"You are an adult, Grace. Pull up your big girl panties." Grace straightened her shoulders, opened the gate, and surged through. Each day during the last week, Cullen had shown he wanted her by word and deed. It was time to trust him. No one could guarantee what happened in the future, so she'd make plans for her business, and in her romantic life, she'd take things one day at a time.

"Cullen," she called, and after a brief tap, she opened the rear door to the kitchen and walked inside. She found him unpacking their meal.

"That smells delicious," she said.

"Do you want wine to go with it?"

"Sounds good."

Cullen brushed a kiss on her temple, the action natural and affectionate. "Take a seat and start while I grab us a drink each."

Grace rubbed at the spot with her fingertips as she stared after him. She loved his... Oh! This was bad. Very bad. How could she have let her emotions get away from her like this? A few weeks ago, she'd thought she'd loved Jeff. Grace mulled over the revelation and decided she'd always loved Cullen. This wasn't a sudden event. She'd always enjoyed his company, and they'd laughed together. They'd always had a friendship, but now it'd deepened to more, and her fears had come to pass.

"Hey!" Cullen returned with two glasses of wine. He placed one in front of her and flicked her chin with his forefinger.

She pulled away and wrinkled her nose at him. "You caught me daydreaming. It's been a long day, and I'm tired."

"Me too," Cullen said. "You'll stay here with me tonight?"

"I'll have to go home to get clothes."

"Why? We'll end up naked anyway, and I have a new toothbrush in the cupboard."

Grace laughed suddenly. *One day at a time.* "We might not get much sleep."

"Count on it," Cullen said with a wink.

They ate their meal together, the conversation flowing easily as it always did between them.

"Josh mentioned he and Ashley are having a barbecue next weekend since his brother- and brother-in-law are coming up from Eketahuna and Moewai. He asked if we'd like to come."

"How could I turn down a barbecue at the prime minister's house?" Grace teased.

"You'll like my friends. Nikolai and Summer aren't far from here. They live in Bottle Top Bay."

"Will we need to take anything? I can bake a cake or something like that."

"I'll tell Josh you're baking a cake," Cullen said. "You can showcase your *New Zealand Best Baker* skills."

Later that night, Grace wandered up the stairs ahead of Cullen and turned into his bedroom.

"Toothbrush," Cullen said. "Flannel for you to wash your face. Do you want me to run next door to get your moisturizer?"

Warmth glowed in Grace. "Thanks. It's on the bathroom counter."

"Where is your key?"

"I didn't lock up."

Cullen frowned. "You probably should. I haven't noticed strangers driving by since we've arrived home, but

I'd take extra precautions for a while. Where are your keys?"

"In my handbag. It's in the bedroom, tucked between the bed and the nightstand."

"I'll lock up for you and bring your handbag."

In five minutes, he was back, and she was ready for bed. She slid beneath the covers and took pleasure in watching Cullen disrobe.

"I enjoy looking at you," she murmured.

He sent her a boyish grin. "Likewise. I adore your curves and the way your breasts overflow my hands."

Cullen pulled back the covers and joined her, drawing her into an embrace. He kissed her softly, starting slow and gradually deepening the contact. He stroked his tongue against hers, enticing her to sink into the kiss with him. His hands stroked and cupped, massaged, and teased until Grace turned into a quivering mass of urgent need.

"Cullen," she whispered against his throat. "Please."

He released her and flopped onto his back. "On top of me, cupcake. I want you to take what you need and give me lots of memories to pull out when we're not together."

Grace frowned. "I'm not very good at this. I always feel clumsy and self-conscious."

"Cupcake." There was a warning in the cutesy nickname.

Grace took heed and decided what the hell. Mostly, Cullen had taken the lead. It might be fun to explore his body and drive him wild with lust. She was positive she could do it.

Without another word, she straddled his lean hips and

grinned down at him. His gaze had attached to her breasts, and she cupped them, plucking at her nipples and teasing herself and him. His erection pressed against her butt, and she wriggled a fraction, letting the slick head slide across her buttock. Cullen groaned, and that was the instant when she decided this was fun. Grace ran her fingers over his bulky chest and explored the dip and swell of his pectoral muscles, the ridges of his abs. She leaned forward to tease his flat nipples with her tongue. He cradled her head, holding her in position and encouraging her to continue. She tested his skin with her mouth and sucked tiny kisses that left a path of red marks going down his rib cage.

"Grace, I like that." Cullen wasn't shy about asking for more. "Harder. Mark me so I can see the signs tomorrow."

She licked, nipped, sucked, and varied the degree of marking. She amused herself by running her tongue down his abs and testing the bulk of his muscles. As she worked her way farther down his body, she stroked his erection with light caresses that didn't come close to the pressure he enjoyed.

"No more teasing," he ordered finally. "Take me inside you. I wanna watch my cock disappear and merge with your flesh. Feel your slickness and the friction when you rise and fall on my dick."

"Yes," she whispered, heat crawling over her chest and neck and flushing her face. While she wanted that desperately, she still took her time. She slid her lips across his, teasing herself as much as him. Her sex tingled, and dampness provided the perfect amount of friction when she rubbed against his cock without allowing penetration. Grace had one more goal before she moved the process along toward the ultimate pleasure. She sucked the swell of a pectoral muscle, purposely making it hard enough to leave a mark.

"Yes," Cullen whispered, and he followed this up with a hoarse groan.

Grace's breasts prickled, and the blissful sensation arced downward to the needy spot between her legs. Okay, she'd lied. There was one more thing she wanted to do. She scooted back down Cullen's body and took his cock into her mouth. With a flick of her tongue, she smoothed away the bead of pre-come that appeared. She licked, letting his taste wind through her senses.

Cullen wove his fingers into her hair and held her in position, silently imploring her to continue. Her tongue rolled over his head and under to tease the delicate underside.

"Yes," he murmured again.

She pulled away with a loud pop that had his eyes flying open, his mouth firming in silent protest.

"I promise I'll do that again, but right now, I'm going to self-combust if I don't get you inside me."

"Thank the lord," he muttered in a heartfelt tone that had her chuckling. That was another thing she adored about being with Cullen—the fun and laughter they experienced while making love and the simple companionship when they were doing ordinary things. He reached over to his bedside drawer and grabbed a condom. Seconds later, he rolled it on with his big hands and sent her an expectant stare.

"Patience," she scolded, wagging a finger at him. She flashed her pussy at Cullen as she positioned herself, then instead of doing as he expected, she held herself above his body and stroked a finger across her needy clit.

"Hmm," she said, repeating the move because it felt so decadent.

Cullen growled. "Cupcake."

A laugh rolled from her in pure delight, and she caressed her clit for a third time, savoring the jolt of enjoyment that slipped through her.

Cullen grasped her hips while amusement filled his eyes. Despite his protests, he was enjoying this as much as her.

Suddenly impatient, Grace positioned his cock and bore down, impaling herself in one quick downward plunge.

"Yes," Cullen hissed.

His shaft filled her, offering exquisite friction and the promise of tremendous pleasure. She lifted her hips and sank back down, experimenting with the pace and angle until she found one she enjoyed. Her eyes slid closed so she could absorb the sensations rushing through her. Her breasts bounced, and her entire body was on display, but she didn't care, not when she hadn't seen a hint of judgment in Cullen's expression. His calm acceptance went a long way to boost her morale, her courage.

"Do you like this position?" he asked. "Because from my perspective, it's a winner. I can hold your breasts and tease those pouty nipples of yours. I can thumb them until they're tight, or I can give you a hint of pain."

"Your expression is amazing," Grace said. "You look at

me as if...as if..."

"As if what, cupcake?"

"As if I'm your everything," she whispered, another flash of heat working down her chest.

"That's because you are," he replied instantly. "I've had plenty of time to imagine myself in this position, plenty of time to plan and decide what it might be like when I'm loving you or when you're taking control and responsibility for our pleasure."

"No pressure," Grace protested.

"Not a bit," he declared. "Just lots of togetherness and trust and the feel-good factor. No, don't stop moving. I want to watch you sway. Your tits move."

Not one of her previous lovers had stated their needs, their wants, their desires while making love. It had always been about getting off as fast as possible. And she'd settled, letting them get away with their shoddy treatment. The realization stung, even if it was the truth. Cullen was their polar opposite.

"Hey!" He pinched her nipple hard, and the resulting pain raced through nerve endings to land in the achy place between her thighs. "Stay with me."

A gasp escaped before she managed, "My mind is firmly on you."

"I thought you'd gone to sleep."

"With you inside me? Never," she said, her tone solemn.

"Minx."

Grace grinned and resumed her rise and fall, still experimenting to get the perfect angle.

"Use your finger because otherwise, I'm going to come

first," Cullen gritted out, no longer displaying the same amusement of seconds earlier.

Grace followed his order and shuddered at the rush of sensation that feathered from her touch. "You'd never leave me hanging," she protested, knowing this with every particle of her being. "You're a generous lover. It gives you joy to see me come and know you played a part."

"Now you're making the *process* feel like a chemical equation." The corners of his eyes crinkled as if he was trying not to laugh.

"I like to see you orgasm," Grace whispered. "It makes me feel powerful and happy and more in control than I've ever been."

"You are a strong woman, Grace. One day, I'd like you to see yourself the way I do. Clever and confident and so skilled with your baking."

"Is that the way to your heart?" she asked, uncomfortable with his words.

"Ah!" he said, his eyes growing dark.

Yet for the life of her, she couldn't read him. The man only gave what he wanted to give, but she didn't fear his shadows. She understood they came from his life experiences, and she'd glimpsed the same quietness in Cullen's friend, Josh.

She lifted and pushed down, filling her needy flesh. Close, but she was happy with the slow build—the tease.

"Not fast enough," Cullen gritted out. He lifted her and turned their bodies before she could blink. He caged her with his arms and his strength, his eyes glowing as he grinned down at her. "You were teasing me."

"Yes."

"Can't have that," he said, but grinning lips—that sexy mouth of his—told her he hadn't truly minded. "What I am is desperate, cupcake." He stroked into her and pulled back, repeating the move in rapid succession.

"Yes. Right there."

"Right there?"

"Cullen!"

His laughter rang out, and then he leaned down to caress her lips with his. "I'm so happy."

"Me too." If he was brave enough to discuss feelings and emotions, then she could too.

He thrust into her again. Once. Twice. Three times, driving her higher each time until she gasped, caught on the edge between pleasure and pain. One last stroke nudged her over the cliff, and she soared, the colors of the sensual celebration bursting behind her closed eyes. Cullen leaned down for a kiss, his tongue stroking against hers in a facsimile of lovemaking. A quiver ran through her, and another small series of spasms had her gasping against Cullen's lips.

"Yes," Cullen muttered, his hands gripping her shoulders hard as he stilled, buried deep inside her. "Grace," he said, seconds before he kissed her again.

Their skin stuck together, and Cullen was becoming a heavy weight across her chest, but she didn't complain, loving the sensation of him holding her down, protecting her, loving her.

As if he read her mind, he broke their kiss and shifted a fraction, rearranging their bodies for comfort.

"Each time we do that, it gets better," Cullen said as he removed the condom.

Grace just grinned. "We're comfortable together. Friends and lovers."

"My point," Cullen said, yawning widely. "That's exactly how it should be between us." His eyes fluttered closed, and he fell asleep.

Grace didn't conk out as fast, her mind busy trying to work out the subtext. What did he mean? Cullen hadn't spoken of the future. Their future. Yes, they were friends, but making love and the intimacy between them now changed everything. It made things far murkier, and despite her promise to herself to live each day, instead of worrying about things she couldn't control, she couldn't see forever happiness ahead.

An ache formed in her chest, and she slammed her eyes shut to halt the heaviness in her heart turning to tears.

One day at a time, dammit.

21

UNWELCOME VISITORS

"I'M GETTING A LOT of crank phone calls," Grace told Cullen five nights later. She and Cullen were sitting on her back deck with a drink each. Bees buzzed around a bed of marigolds, but the day's summer heat had dispersed, and a pleasant breeze wafted from the west. "They say nothing, but I can hear them breathing on the other end of the call."

"Have you tried calling the number back?"

"No, because I don't know the identity of my caller. I figured it was better not to engage. I've blocked two numbers so far, but I keep getting the calls. If it's a telemarketer, they speak to you. It doesn't feel like that."

Cullen straightened in his chair, his gaze intent and a frown forming on his forehead. "Have you noticed anything weird around the house? Strange cars driving past?"

"Work has taken most of my time, but nothing has stuck

out as unusual. What about you? Did you see anything odd?"

"No, and I've been looking," Cullen said. "The shoes hanging in the tree have gone. I figured that with the dirtbag in custody, everything was back to normal."

Grace shrugged. "Maybe it is nothing. Can you light the barbecue for me? I'll get the steaks."

They'd just finished dinner when Cullen's phone rang.

"Hey, Josh." Cullen listened for a few minutes. "No, I can meet you there. You give me instructions, and I'll do the work. See you in ten minutes."

"Problem?" Grace asked when Cullen ended the call.

"Yeah, a property Josh monitors has a problem. He needs me to help him since he can't work with his arm."

"You want to get out of doing the dishes."

Cullen grinned and drew her into an embrace. "Ya got me." He kissed the tip of her nose. "I've no idea what time I'll be home, but I have a key. Make sure you lock up."

"Promise."

Five minutes later, Cullen had left to meet Josh. Grace cleaned up their dinner mess before deciding to watch a movie and ponder her business ideas. Cakes or special bakes for Valentine's Day appealed to her. That way, she could experiment. She grabbed her phone to do a search on Valentine's Day cakes.

The front doorbell halted her internet search, and she paused the movie and stood to answer the summons, slipping the phone into the pocket of her sundress. The bell rang a second time, along with a knock. Grace opened the door to find two burly suit-wearing men. One had a shaved head while the other had such short hair he might as well have been bald. The pair towered over her, their faces set in impassive expressions.

She didn't know them, hadn't seen them before, but the hair lifted on her nape, and instinct had her slamming the door shut. She didn't get far. One man stuck his foot in the gap, his bulk preventing her from placing the door between them.

"What do you want?" she snapped.

"Our boss wants to speak with you," Shaved Head said in a low rumble.

"He didn't think of calling or sending an email or text?" Grace snapped before she thought better of it.

"Miss, our boss doesn't like to be kept waiting."

"Why does he want to talk to me? Who is he? What have I done?" Grace asked.

"Miss," Short Hair broke in on her rapid-fire questions. "Our boss has a temper, and he's already angry with your boyfriend." He grasped her upper arm and dragged her through the doorway before she could resist. "You're coming with us now."

It was like an ant facing off with an elephant. Grace had no alternative but to go with them. Outside, darkness had fallen, the streetlights automatically switching on and bathing the street in a cobweb of light and shadows.

Julia, her neighbor and the woman she'd discovered with Jeff, walked past with her Labrador.

"Help!" Grace shrieked.

Julia continued walking. She didn't even glance in Grace's direction.

"Bitch," Grace muttered.

Shaved Head laughed. "Didn't expect she'd help. That one is only interested in herself." He opened the rear door of a large steel-gray Chrysler and waited for her to get inside.

Grace darted away, her hand going to her phone. Her glance down to speed dial Cullen was her undoing.

Short Hair grasped her shoulder and spun her around, but she hit the number and slipped the phone back into her pocket before he grabbed her.

"Stop mucking around," he snapped. "You're coming with us."

"I'm going with you against my will." Grace spoke loudly and clearly, hoping that Cullen might pick up some of the conversation. "I'm a sane person, and I don't want to go with two strangers to meet someone I don't know."

Short Hair propelled her into the vehicle and closed the door behind her.

The two men climbed into the front, and the doors locked.

"Put on your seatbelt," Shaved Hair ordered.

"Great. I get kidnapped and have a safety-conscious abductor," Grace said.

Short Hair sniggered but put on his belt.

"Stop mucking around," Shaved Head snarled at Grace. "Put on the damn seatbelt. You've created a lot of trouble for our boss, and you're lucky he's being polite about having a meeting with you."

"This is polite?" Grace shrieked. She glowered at the rear-vision mirror, her gaze connecting with Shaved

Head's. What she saw in his eyes made her decide to cooperate. She clicked the seatbelt into place.

Soon they were on their way, but Grace was none the wiser.

"Where are we going? Can you at least tell me that?" She continued to speak loudly, hoping Cullen had received her call and was listening. If he wasn't, she didn't know what she'd do.

Short Hair sighed. "We're driving into the city to the Hobson Apartments. Now, will you shut up?"

"The Hobson Apartments? Aren't they luxury apartments worth over five million each? Exactly who is your boss?"

"Button it!" Shaved Hair ordered. "Do I have to show you my gun?"

Until now, she'd been too angry for fear, but the mention of a gun had her freezing, her mouth open. She swallowed back the words pushing and shoving for release, and pressed her lips together. *Please, please let Cullen have heard part of the conversation because she had a terrible feeling about this situation.*

Cullen absently answered his phone while waiting for Josh to finish his call to Nikolai. What he heard made his chest grow cold and fear to grip him in sharp talons. He signaled to Josh and pressed a finger to his lips, indicating Josh should listen but not talk. Once they heard the mention of Hobson Apartments, Josh stepped away and spoke to Nikolai in a low voice. He hung up and gestured for Cullen to follow him.

At Cullen's vehicle, he handed over his phone to Josh to listen to Grace. Once they were both in the SUV, Cullen tore out of the parking lot, his pulse racing.

He couldn't lose Grace. Not now. He'd always liked her, and now those feelings had solidified into love. He hadn't told Grace in words, but he hoped he'd shown her in deed how much he cared for her. Until he completed his last mission, he couldn't in good conscience commit to Grace. His hands clenched the wheel. No, that wasn't the truth. He was committed to Grace now. He wanted everything with her. A marriage. A family. A dog or a cat. Maybe both.

The trip to the Hobson didn't take long since they were already in the city for Josh's work crisis. He and Josh exited the vehicle. Josh handed Cullen's phone to him while Josh called Nikolai again.

Josh signaled five minutes to Cullen, and he nodded. He continued to listen to Grace.

She cleared her throat. "Are you sure you can't tell me who I'm going to see against my will?" Her voice trembled, and Cullen vowed to thump whoever had instilled that fear in her.

"No." The terse reply didn't help Cullen.

"Who lives in apartment six?" Grace's voice wavered while Cullen saluted her bravery. She was trusting him to help her, and he wouldn't fail this wonderful woman.

His woman.

He heard a sharp rap on a door filter down the line and Grace's soft gasp.

"Go in there and wait for the boss," a voice growled.

A vehicle pulled up, and Nikolai, Louie, and Jake

climbed out along with another guy that Cullen didn't recognize and a woman. They headed directly for Cullen and Josh.

"Josh. Cullen." Jake nodded at them. "This is my buddy, Luke. He's from Sloan and is a cop like me. This is Janaya, his wife."

"Hi." Cullen put the phone down against his side and spoke in a low voice. "They've gone to apartment six. Grace is in a room waiting for the boss to show up."

"Apartment six is Matthew Geraghty, the hotshot lawyer. They say he's worth a few billion these days," Josh said. "And lucky for you, I did the security there six months ago. The guy got me to do the job because of Ashley." He let his disgust show. "As if I'd ever try to get Ashley to do any favors for my customers."

"Right, we know where she is," Cullen said. "Can we please get my lady?"

"Weapons?" Nikolai asked.

"I don't have my gun," Josh said. "Not that I'm much help with my arm."

"I'm not armed either," Cullen replied.

"Probably best if we keep the weapons to a minimum," Luke said. "There are six of us."

"They have two goons plus the lawyer. The lawyer won't want to get his hands dirty," Cullen said.

"Any idea what this is about?" Nikolai asked.

"Grace's ex sold drugs. He's in custody now, awaiting charges, and the drug supply is also with the cops. I'm guessing there are more drugs somewhere, and the lawyer and his organization want them back. It's only a guess. I don't care what he wants. Grace is an innocent in this, and she doesn't deserve the crap her ex has heaped on her."

"Let's go," Josh said. "I'll knock on the door. If the goons are standing outside, I'll distract them while you guys immobilize them. Ride up to the fifth floor, then take the stairs to the sixth."

"Let Janaya go with you," Luke suggested. "She has worked as a bodyguard, and they won't suspect anything dire if a man and woman come to their door. Between you, cause a disturbance."

"Thanks." Cullen would take all the help he could get. If Jake hadn't objected to the proposed plan, Cullen figured Luke spoke the truth about his wife's capabilities. He raised the phone to his ear and listened. He heard nothing, and his guts twisted in knots. Grace had to be all right.

A masculine voice spoke, rich with a trace of arrogance. "Ms. Feeney. You have led me a merry dance." The man projected his voice, so Cullen heard him clearly. No doubt his courtroom appearances had honed his speaking skills.

We're coming, cupcake. Keep him talking as long as possible.

As if she heard him, Grace said, "I'm sorry, but I don't know who you are or why you ordered your heavies to collect me like an unwanted package. I am a baker. I'm not used to men forcing me into a car."

"Did they hurt you?"

"They threatened me with a gun when I kept asking questions," Grace snapped. "Why am I here, and who the hell are you?"

Cullen listened and scrambled into the elevator with the

other men. None of them spoke. On the fifth floor, they piled off the car, leaving Josh and Janaya to travel to the sixth floor.

Cullen's insides twisted again, and fear slithered down his backbone. What if he didn't make it in time and this lawyer hurt Grace? Damn it, if—no when—he got his hands on Grace again, he intended to ask her to marry him. He'd go back to the war zone an engaged man if he had anything to do with it. He wanted to ensure Grace understood he cared for her. That he was committed and would never cheat on her. *She* was the woman he wanted.

Cullen double-timed it up the concrete stairs and slid open the door at the top. He peered out into the corridor on the sixth level and spotted Josh and Janaya speaking to two immense men in suits. He blinked as Janaya whipped a weapon out of her dress pocket and jammed it in the ribs of a man with a bald head. Baldy dropped like a stone. Before the second man could react, he suffered the same fate.

The instant he slid to the ground, Cullen was through the doorway and jogging down the passage to join Josh and Janaya.

"That's my girl," Luke said.

"I loathe bullies," Janaya said, her violet eyes narrowed. "You know that."

Josh tried the door to the apartment. "Locked," he said. "Check them for keys."

Janaya squatted beside the bald man and rifled his pockets. Cullen checked the second man and produced a set of keys.

"Which key, Josh?"

"Let me," Josh said, snatching the keys from his palm. Seconds later, they'd unlocked the door, opened it enough to slide through into the apartment. They communicated in hand signals, slipping into the apartment one after the other.

A gravelly voice rose and fell from a room to the right. "Ms. Feeney, you have something that belongs to me."

22

RESCUE

GRACE SWALLOWED HARD, HER gaze running over the casually clad man before scanning the rest of the room. Behind the man, large glass windows overlooked the central business district and the harbor beyond. The city lights sparkled and glowed like gorgeous jewels. She noted the room contents—the expensive wooden furniture and the thick cream carpet beneath her feet. A massive modern painting provided a burst of red and green and yellow and blue—the only actual color in the room.

"Did you hear me, Ms. Feeney?"

"I heard you," Grace snapped. "And I have no clue what you mean. I don't know who the hell you think you are, but you have no right to detain me. I'm leaving, Mr. Whoever-You-Are."

"Matthew Geraghty," the man said, a strange note in his voice.

SHELLEY MUNRO

"Well, Mr. Geraghty, please speak plainly and tell me exactly what you want. I'm terrible at guessing games."

"Your fiancé, Jeff Howard, took four statues from me. I wish their return."

"He's not my fiancé. I kicked him out and severed our connection when I discovered him having sex with another woman in my bed. I don't have the statues. I threw them out on the side of the road with the rest of Jeff's belongings." She decided it best not to mention the royal salute gnome because that was safe with the cops.

"You're telling the truth."

"Yes," Grace barked.

The man's eyes widened, and his hand went to his hip.

"I wouldn't do that if I were you," Cullen's voice sounded from behind her.

Grace spun around, her mouth dropping open on seeing the four men and one woman standing with Cullen. She didn't recognize any of them, but they held their weapons with easy confidence. Even the woman with her long blonde hair and unusual violet eyes looked as if she knew what to do with the strange gun in her hands.

"Cupcake, get behind me," Cullen said in an even voice.

Grace raced to obey, never so pleased to see anyone in all her life. "Thank you," she said as she circled the strangers and stood behind Cullen.

"Grace doesn't have your statues. She dumped the scumbag's clothes on the footpath and left them for him to collect. How could she know he was running drugs from her house? She's the innocent in this situation. I suggest if you want your statues, you go after the moron."

"He's in protected custody," Geraghty said.

"Not my problem," Cullen said. "You will leave Grace out of this situation of yours, otherwise you will face the consequences."

"I can see that," the man gritted out.

Grace peered around Cullen's bulk and witnessed the man's frustration.

"We'll be going now," Cullen said. "I mean it. Leave Grace alone. If you keep out of her way, we'll back off and leave you to your own devices. If you don't..." Cullen trailed off.

The blonde woman spoke. "You might have money and power. A workforce to do your bidding, but that won't keep you safe if you go after Cullen's lady. Got it?"

"Yes," Geraghty snapped.

Cullen's lady. The words warmed her through and left her almost giddy with delight.

"Let's go." Cullen guided Grace from the apartment where she discovered Josh monitoring the two men who'd driven her here.

"Josh," Grace exclaimed.

"Glad to see you're okay," Josh said with an affable grin.

"Are they all right?" Grace asked, looking down at Short Hair and Shaved Head.

"They might wake up with a headache, but other than that, they'll be fine," Josh replied.

Cullen's arm tightened around her waist. "Are you okay?" His warm breath feathered across her ear.

"I am now that you're here. Is it possible to be both scared and angry?"

Cullen grunted as he guided her toward the lift. "Yes."

Once they crowded into the lift, Cullen ran through the introductions. "This is Nikolai, Josh's brother-in-law, Jake, Louie, and this is Luke and Janaya, who are both friends of Jake's."

"Thank you so much for coming to my aid," Grace said.

"A little excitement to add to our city visit," Janaya said with a friendly smile.

"I've been experimenting with cakes to bake for Valentine's Day," Grace said. "Could I thank you all with cake and coffee?"

"Grace was on the *New Zealand Best Baker* show," Cullen said. "She makes excellent cakes."

ALMOST TWO HOURS LATER, Grace and Cullen showed their guests out. Cullen curved his arm around her waist, and he held her against his side, glorying in her touch. Her presence.

"I like your friends very much," Grace said as they watched the men and Janaya pile into the two vehicles and drive away. "I can't wait to meet their wives. If my boss wants me to work on Saturday, I'm going to tell her no."

Cullen squeezed her and turned Grace so he could look into her eyes. "Cupcake, I love you. I swear I aged ten years when your call came through."

"Cullen," she whispered with something like hope in her gaze.

Cullen ushered her inside, out of the way of prying eyes,

and closed the door. He hadn't wanted to propose when he mightn't return home. A poor choice, and he was about to make that right. He inhaled and exhaled, seeking to calm his racing pulse as nerves struck.

"Grace, I do love you. So damn much. I'd thought that once it's time for me to return to my unit, I'd ask you to wait for me. Tonight..." His hands tightened on her shoulders. Things could've gone bad if he hadn't reached her in time. "Tonight showed me that waiting is crazy. I want to marry you, Grace, if you'll have me."

Her face crumpled, and she burrowed against his chest, leaving him anxious and confused.

"Cupcake, talk to me."

"I didn't think you wanted me that way." She lifted her pale face, and the tears glinting in her green eyes almost took him out at the knees.

"I want everything with you," he gritted out. "Our present. Our future. A home. A family. Everything. Grace, will you please marry me and make me the happiest man alive?"

"Are you sure?"

"I have never been more positive of anything in my life." Cullen's chest tightened, and his breathing sped up as he waited for her to speak.

A smile dawned on her face, growing brighter and brighter until it reached her gorgeous eyes. "Yes. If you're certain."

"Tell me you love me," he demanded.

"Cullen, I do love you. More than anything, but I assumed you wanted something temporary until you returned to your soldiering."

"I've wanted you for years. Ask Josh. When you walked into the pub that day after finding the ratfink with Julia, I was busy drinking away my sorrows. I'd decided to make my move during this holiday, but then you divulged your marriage plans. It was the worst day of my life until you walked into the pub."

Grace beamed and stood on tiptoe to kiss him. Cullen lifted her and strolled toward the stairs without separating their mouths.

Grace gasped. "Cullen, where are we going?"

"I am going to take my fiancée to bed, and tomorrow, we're going ring shopping. I want every other man out there to know you're taken." He adjusted her position, so he cradled her against his chest and climbed the stairs to his bedroom.

"Isn't that a bit cave-mannish?"

"Too bad. Grace, I still have to return to my unit. I can't leave until my term with the army ends."

Grace sobered as he set her on her feet. "I understand."

"While I'm gone, you'll have the support of Josh and his wife. My other friends."

"The prime minister will be too busy to watch over me," Grace replied tartly.

Cullen laughed. "I said the support. If I know Summer and the other women, they'll invite you to go out with them and include you in their activities. They're good people, Grace. And once I get home, we'll get married. Okay?"

Grace lifted her hands to cup his face. "I'd like that

very much. While you're away, we'll still be able to communicate, speak on the phone, and email?"

"Yes."

"Then it's settled. We'll get married once you get home. Something quiet and intimate. I want something different from the last fiasco."

"Done," Cullen said, and he set about kissing her and removing Grace's clothes. She laughingly tried to help him undress too, and their hands, heads, and other body parts kept colliding. Laughter rang out, and Cullen smiled so wide his mouth hurt.

Finally, they were both naked, and they toppled to the bed. Cullen caged Grace in his arms and grinned down at her. "I love you so much, cupcake. You've made this soldier happy. So happy."

Grace met his hungry kiss with equal passion, and they didn't surface for a long, long time.

EPILOGUE

THE TROPICAL AIR WAS full of flowers and spices, while the surroundings were bright with pink hibiscus and lush greenery. On the white sandy beach, coconut palms rustled faintly in the breeze. Grace had never visited Fiji before, but she was a fan, especially now that her fiancé stood at her side. He'd flown directly from wherever he'd been, meeting her and their friends at the hotel yesterday.

After her last wedding drama, she'd worried Cullen might not arrive, but he'd tapped on their bedroom door last night looking tired but healthy and happy. Her body tingled with the residual aches of lovemaking. She'd missed Cullen so much during their months of separation, but Cullen's friends had helped to keep her sanity intact.

And now he was here.

He stood beside her, beneath a flower-bedecked shelter with Grace's parents and dozens of their friends.

"Do you take this man to be your husband?" A

tall Fijian marriage celebrant, dressed in pristine white, conducted the ceremony.

"I do," Grace said without hesitation. She exchanged a loving smile with her almost husband.

"Do you promise to love and honor him?"

"I will," Grace said. "I might even obey him sometimes."

Laughter rippled from those standing around them to witness their nuptials.

The celebrant's lips twitched, but he continued with the vows.

"I do," Cullen said.

"Now, with the power vested in me, I pronounce you man and wife. You may kiss your bride."

Cullen's arms came around her, and he kissed her. Soft at first, but with growing passion. Wolf whistles rang out, along with clapping and cheering.

"Hey! Enough of that," Summer shouted. "It's time for photos."

"Have you noticed Summer is always spoiling the celebration kiss with her need to take photos?" Josh commented in a loud carrying complaint.

Cullen chuckled at Grace's side. "So I've heard. I missed Josh's wedding and Matt's too. In our defense, Grace and I haven't seen each other for six months."

"We're sticking with tradition," Summer defended herself. "Photos, followed by lazing around the pool or on the beach. The beach, since the tide is coming in, then we'll dance and eat and make merry."

Grace leaned closer to Cullen. "I don't mind what we do, as long as we have private time together. I've missed you."

"We'll need to change before we go to the beach," Cullen whispered. "We'll make a start on our honeymoon then."

"I can't wait for that part of our marriage."

"Are you sure you want to start a family straight away?" Cullen asked, still keeping his voice low. "I know we've discussed it during our online chats and in emails, but if you've changed your mind, that's all right too. We have time. Your happiness is a bigger priority than my need for a family."

"I love you, Cullen," Grace said, her chest squeezing with a wealth of emotion. "How about we let nature take its course and go from there?"

He turned her to face him. "No birth control?"

"No birth control," she confirmed.

Despite the exodus toward the beach for photos, Cullen took her in his arms and kissed her soundly. "I have missed this, cupcake. The video calls were great, but there is no substitute for touching you, kissing you."

"Ahem!" a loud feminine voice said from behind them.

Grace and Cullen turned to see Summer with her camera. They grinned, and she clicked the shutter.

"That's a goodie," Summer said after peering at her screen. "Come down to the beach. I know you haven't seen each other for months, but everyone is waiting."

"Are you ready, Mrs. Turner?" Cullen asked, his eyes twinkling at her.

Grace jolted. "Oh, right. That's me." Chagrined, she said. "Mr. Turner and I are ready to do this photo thing."

The afternoon passed with much laughter and teasing. After a buffet dinner, with an island flavor, they and their group danced under the moonlight. Then, they called their goodnights, and hand-in-hand, she and Cullen left to go to their room.

Cullen closed the door behind them and locked it with a loud click. "I can't stop grinning," he said. "I can hardly believe we're married."

Grace pinched his biceps.

"What was that for?" he asked.

"I have to keep touching you to reassure myself you're here."

"I am very much here." He rubbed his lower body against her, and she laughed.

"Ready for the honeymoon phase?"

"I've been dreaming of holding you in my arms again. Last night barely dented my need."

Grace pulled from his touch and presented her back to him. "Unfasten my dress for me."

"You've lost weight, cupcake," he said.

"I've been racing around a lot, trying to get my orders done before having to fly to Fiji. Summer and Ashley helped me to do the last of the deliveries." She laughed as she stepped out of her dress. "Ashley was a big hit. My customers loved chatting with the prime minister, although I had to tell them this wouldn't be an ongoing business feature. Usually, Ashley is way too busy to deliver cakes!"

"Stop," Cullen said. "I'll take care of the rest of your clothing. Did I tell you how beautiful you looked today?

Now?"

"Thank you. I've never been so happy. I'm married to the man I love, and thanks to you, I have this wonderful network of friends who pitch in and help if I need it."

"Word is you've been doing a little babysitting in exchange," Cullen said. "As much as the guys adore their kids, they enjoy having quiet time with their wives. They told me you were a natural with kids." He tweaked her nose. "I already knew that from personal experience."

Grace sat to unfasten her shoes.

"Let me be your Prince Charming," he said.

Once he'd removed her shoes, he rose and discarded every scrap of his clothing.

"Cullen," Grace murmured.

"Yes, Mrs. Turner?"

"Make love to me."

They sank onto the bed together, hands stroking and caressing.

Cullen lifted his head after feasting on her mouth for long moments. "As much as I have enjoyed seeing you in this sexy lingerie, I want to see and touch what is beneath this white silk and lace." He unfastened her bra and kissed a trail down her belly before he dragged down her lacy white panties. He kissed each inch of skin he'd exposed, so the process took some time.

"You're my wife," Cullen murmured seconds before he parted her legs and kissed the heart of her. He licked along her slit, making her moan. "Each time I look at you, I want to shout and cheer and tell everyone you're mine."

Although her doubts had faded during the months

since they first got together, it was nice to hear his words, especially since he echoed her thoughts.

"I'm the lucky one," she whispered. "Come up here and kiss me."

"I haven't finished exploring my gorgeous wife yet," he said.

"Cullen." Her voice emerged sharp and decisive. "You did lots of exploring last night. Please, I feel empty. Fill me. Take me for the first time as your wife. I ache for you."

He grinned, and although he bore shadows beneath his eyes from lack of sleep, satisfaction and contentment radiated from him. "Since you put it that way."

Cullen rose up her body and placed his weight on his hands as he stared down at her. He kissed her lips slowly and tenderly before nudging her thighs farther apart.

He reached over to the nightstand.

"What are you doing?" she asked.

"Condom," he murmured against her mouth.

"No condom, remember?"

He laughed. "I forgot. It's an ingrained habit. I've never had sex without a condom."

"It will be a first for both of us."

Cullen lined up and slid his cock into her. "Wow," he murmured. "You feel amazing. There's more heat, and the friction is incredible."

"Yes," Grace said with a gasp.

She clutched his shoulders and held tight, meeting each of his strokes with a rise of her hips. "Yes, right there." She sucked in a breath as pleasure shimmered through her. "I love you, Cullen. So much. It's great to have you home."

"I was counting the days," he said.

"Enough talking," she muttered, wriggling a fraction.

He thrust smoothly into her, repeating the strokes and going faster and faster until they were both breathing hard and clinging to each other. Grace met each thrust with enthusiasm, glorying in his touch, her rising pleasure, and their joyful joining. Their marriage.

"Cullen, I love you," she cried, and seconds later, she soared into toe-tingling, glorious bliss. "Yes!"

Cullen released a strangled chuckle, his body weighing her down in the best possible way. He pushed into her again. Once. Twice. On the third deep surge, he stilled, and she felt the throb of his cock. Her channel twitched and tightened, a zing of sensation taking her by surprise. Then Cullen was kissing her and rolling them, so she sprawled on top of him. His hands skimmed her back and cupped her butt, sending a shiver of delight through her.

"I think I like this marriage business," Cullen murmured.

"Only think?"

"It's still new, but the sex is spectacular," he said, kissing her again.

"I agree with everything you say," Grace said with a loud yawn.

Cullen swatted her on the butt. "An auspicious start to our marriage, then. If you keep agreeing with my every word, we'll be sweet."

"You realize Summer and my other friends will lead me astray."

Cullen lifted his head to grin, his happiness and the

genuine love displayed on his face stealing her breath. "Nikolai, backed by the other men, informed me make-up sex was excellent and that a good argument never hurt a marriage.

Grace blinked. "You got marriage advice?"

"Don't tell me the wives didn't give you pearls of wisdom, too."

His broad grin had her smiling in return, and she cupped his handsome face. Now that he'd left the army, he'd relaxed more, and she'd never seen him smile as often. It was a good look for him.

"They couldn't help themselves," she said with a dry smile.

"That's what I thought," he said, his expression turning smug. A hint of curiosity crept over his face. "So what will you do?"

"That's a simple question," Grace said. "I'm going to love you as hard as I can and enjoy the hell out of every day, every hour, every moment we have together."

Cullen stared at her, then gave a decisive nod. "Works for me," he said, and he settled in to kiss her senseless. Again.

WANT A PEEK AT Cullen's and Grace's Future?

Not quite ready to let Cullen and Grace go? Me neither. Subscribe to my newsletter, and receive a copy of the bonus story: *Surprise!*

Go here to subscribe and receive your free bonus story: https://BookHip.com/ZVNXLGS

About Author

USA Today bestselling author Shelley Munro lives in Auckland, the City of Sails, with her husband and a cheeky Jack Russell/mystery breed dog.

Typical New Zealanders, Shelley and her husband left home for their big OE soon after they married (translation of New Zealand speak - big overseas experience). A twelve-month-long adventure lengthened to six years of roaming the world. Enduring memories include being almost sat on by a mountain gorilla in Rwanda, lazing on white sandy beaches in India, whale watching in Alaska, searching for leprechauns in Ireland, and dealing with ghosts in an English pub.

While travel is still a big attraction, these days Shelley is most likely found in front of her computer following another love - that of writing stories of contemporary and paranormal romance and adventure. Other interests include watching rugby (strictly for research purposes), cycling, playing croquet and the ukelele, and curling up with an enjoyable book.

Visit Shelley at her Website
https://shelleymunro.com

Join Shelley's Newsletter
https://shelleymunro.com/newsletter

ALSO BY SHELLEY

Military Men
Innocent Next Door
Soldier with Benefits
Safeguarding Sorrel
Stranded with Ella
Josh's Fake Fiancee
Operation Flower Petal
Protecting the Bride

Friendship Chronicles
Secret Lovers
Reunited Lovers
Clandestine Lovers
Part-Time Lovers
Enemy Lovers
Maverick Lovers
Sports Lovers

Fancy Free
Protection
Romp
Buzz
Festive

Single Titles
One Night of Misbehavior
Playing to Win
Reformed Bad Girl

www.ingramcontent.com/pod-product-compliance
Lightning Source LLC
Chambersburg PA
CBHW031211260626
47169CB00007B/2024